PRAIRIE SOUND

PRIMROSE SERIES
BOOK FIVE

TANYA RENEE

Serenade Publishing

www.serenadepublishing.com

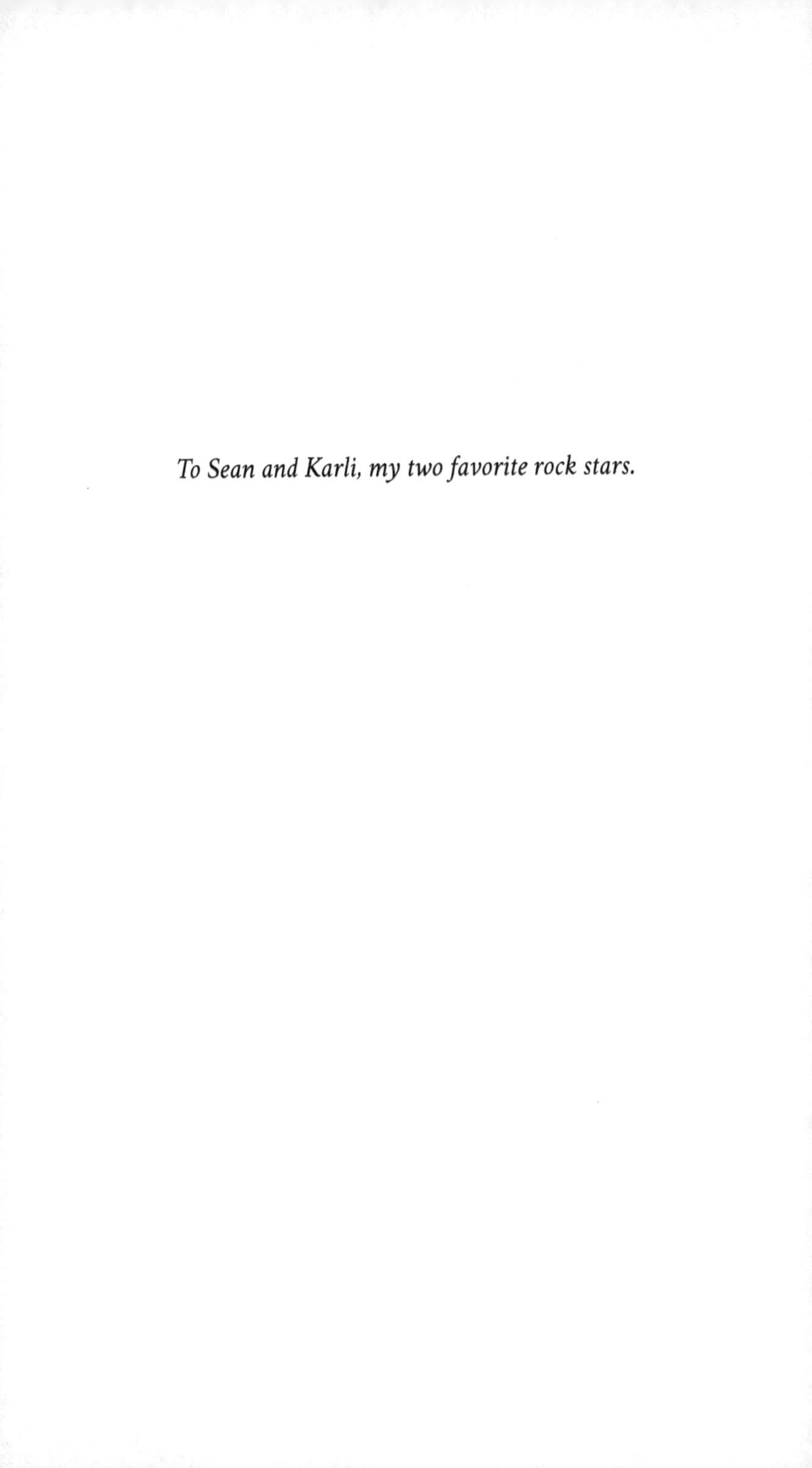

To Sean and Karli, my two favorite rock stars.

ALSO BY TANYA RENEE

Primrose Series

Prairie Sky

Prairie Nights

Prairie Fire

Prairie Hearts

Prairie Sound

PROLOGUE

Staring out at the tranquil water, Savanah Smithfield dangled her feet over the edge of the dock. Dipping her toe into the warm lake, she watched as the water traveled in soft ripples across the surface. A crescent moon shone brightly above her, its reflection shimmering in the water. The sound of crickets chirping, and a cool nighttime breeze rustling the trees, were the only sounds across Camp Clearwater.

Savanah looked down at her watch. 1:32 a.m. He was late. She was breaking curfew and would get into trouble if she was caught. She didn't care. This was the last night of Summer Camp, and she wasn't about to miss their annual rendezvous. It had been an incredible three weeks, and this was her last late-night meetup with her long-time camp friend, Ramiro Perez.

Having met when they were nine years old, for five years, they attended summer camp together. Every year on the last night, they would sneak out of their bunkhouses and meet on the dock to star gaze. Rami had always been easy to talk to, had funny stories about his big Mexican family, and the fun antics and he and his friends got into. They shared many interests and became friends quickly. Every year, Savanah couldn't wait to see him again and catch up.

As she waited on the dock for him, she couldn't help but think about how different and special this Summer had been. This would be their last year at summer camp, and the thought of that made her melancholy. Thinking back on the camp friends she had made over the years; there wasn't even a question that she would miss Rami the most. Perhaps it was all those years, bonding over hikes, archery, or paddling on the lake together in a canoe, but he was her summertime constant and part of the reason she kept coming back to Camp Clearwater, year after year. However, this year, gone was the skinny dark-haired boy she first met, replaced by a handsome teenager, with dark curly shoulder length hair and a tall, lean build. Honestly, she wouldn't have recognized him if it weren't for his endearing lopsided smile she knew so well. He had grown up and she, as a teenage girl, had noticed.

She sighed, thinking about Rami and the talent show that was always held on the last day of camp. When he got up on stage in front of everyone with his guitar and started playing and singing an acoustic version of her favorite Coldplay song, "Sky Full of Stars", she was entranced. As she watched him, his voice, so smooth and rich, her heart did a flip-flop, and butterflies took flight in her belly. His eyes darted around the room until he found her in the crowd. When their gazes met his eyes softened and he flashed her his signature smile making her internally swoon. *Do I have a crush on Rami?* The feelings inside her were something new and unexpected.

The crack of a twig behind her broke her from her thoughts as the sound of heavy footsteps on the wooden planks of the dock made her turn. Rami's handsome smile greeted her, his chocolate brown eyes twinkling in the moonlight.

"Sorry. It took forever for everyone to fall asleep," he said, taking a seat next to her. "I was hoping you would wait for me."

Savanah met his gaze and smiled, an unexpected nervousness rising within her at his proximity to her. To disguise the feeling of awkward awareness, she whispered. "You were awesome tonight."

"Thanks. I'm starting a band with a couple of friends of mine when I get back."

"Really? That's so cool. You know the song you sang tonight is my all-time favorite song," she shared, giving him a sideways glance, and shyly looking back down at her hands.

"I know," he replied, nudging her with his shoulder. "I sang it for you."

With surprise, Savanah looked up, meeting his milk chocolate eyes, and asked, "You did?"

Rami tentatively reached for her hand, threading his fingers with hers, the warmth radiating from him, creating a whirlwind of emotions Savanah had never felt before. She glanced down at their joined hands and slowly back up to meet his stare. A nervous energy surrounded them, and Rami noticeably swallowed it back as he confessed, "I like you, Savanah."

Her eyes searched his sincere and earnest face, her heartbeat quickening as she admitted, "I like you too, Rami."

He reached over and tucked a stray strand of her blonde hair behind her ear, his fingertips lingering on her cheek in a tender caress, making her close her eyes with his timid yet sweet touch.

"Can I kiss you?" he asked, his voice nervously trembling with the question.

Savanah opened her eyes, meeting his hopeful gaze. She had never kissed a boy before, but if there was any boy, she would want to kiss, it would be Rami. She swallowed down, her heart thrumming wildly in her chest as she answered in a breathy whisper, "Yes."

Rami slowly leaned in, his breath smelling fresh like mint, and she closed her eyes in anticipation. His pillowy soft lips brushed against hers, sweet and gentle. A sensation sparked across her body and a warm flush settled in her cheeks as their lips moved slowly over each other's. Pulling apart, their eyes opening slowly, Rami turned quickly, staring out over the water and let out an exhalation he was holding. Savanah glanced to the side, touched her cheek, which was flaming with heat as a smile tugged at her lips. Their eyes slowly met again, and they both offered each other shy smiles. Rami gave her hand a squeeze as they both turned, looking up at the brilliant night sky, relishing their last night under the stars.

CHAPTER 1

Savanah Smithfield prided herself on curating all things pretty. Whether it was dresses, shoes, or jewelry, she loved it all. Fashion was her jam and having her own boutique was a dream come true. At 23 she had accomplished more than most her age. She had a success-ful, albeit short modeling career, had graduated from business school and had acquired this little boutique in a bustling part of downtown St. Augustine. Pretty Things was her passion, what got her up in the morning and what made her fall asleep at night, happy and content. She loved everything about it and couldn't imagine doing anything else.

Even though her passion for what she did gave her purpose, she knew she worked too much. Most young women her age were out and about partying and dating while she spent her evenings in her little townhome, curled up with a romance novel and a glass of wine. It wasn't that she never went out. She had friends but preferred a simple lunch or coffee date or perhaps a quiet gathering at home rather than a late night out on the town.

As for dating, she had a handful of first dates under her belt, but not a lot of potential for anything more. In her limited experienced men seemed hesitant to ask her out and the ones that did came across as superficial. Seeing only her face and not wanting to get to know her personality or appreciate her intelligence.

It was not lost on Savanah that she would be considered pretty. Tall, and willowy in stature, with long silky straight hair, large blue eyes framed with long thick lashes, naturally clear skin dappled with endearing freckles and full pink lips. She was very aware of the glances she got. But Savanah wanted to be known for more than just her pretty face, and that was part of the reason she gave up her modeling career.

Discovered at 15, she saw modeling as a way she could earn some money for college, perhaps travel, and get herself some nice things. She was able to do that and had saved most of the money she had earned. By the time she was 20, the scene got old. She was tired of traveling, tired of the fashion shows, tired of the photo shoots, and mostly she was tired of the sketchy people that seemed to seep into the scene. She wanted a regular life, surrounded by regular people, and she missed home. So, she left that world behind and never looked back. Besides, she hated people telling her what to wear, how to look, and what she should or shouldn't eat. The first things she did when she left modeling were dye her hair cotton candy pink and eat a big sloppy cheeseburger. Three years later, she had no regrets.

"Hey, what are you doing this weekend?" her best friend, Devine "Dee" Jones, asked, combing through the clothing racks.

"I'm going to a celebration for Bea and Garrett. It's sort of a birthday/engagement party." Savanah answered, leaning over the front counter. "It's at the Blue Corn."

"Oh, I love that place!" Dee replied, as she sifted through a rack of clothes, sizing as she went. "I still can't believe Garrett is getting married again. Your brother is such a nice guy. I'm so happy for him."

"Yes, me too! His fiancé, Bea, is awesome, and Amelia adores her. I'm just so happy he's found someone so amazing." Savanah said dreamily, as a little giggle escaped her lips. "You should see him, Dee. He is completely head over heels."

Dee placed her hand over her heart. "That's so sweet." She cooed, turning the conversation to Savanah. "How about you? Any prospects I need to know about?" Dee asked, tucking her crochet braids behind her ear as she continued sorting.

Savanah sighed with exasperation and answered with a question, "What prospects?"

Dee rolled her eyes and gave her a chiding side eye. "You know, you can't meet someone unless you leave your house, right?"

"I leave my house!" Savanah protested. "I come to work, I go grocery shopping, I..."

Dee held up her hand and pinned her friend with her stare. "Savanah, you never socialize."

"I know, I know," Savanah responded, aware of her introverted tendencies then added, "I'm going to a concert this weekend though. Bea, Garrett, and a couple of their friends are going to see this popular local rock band."

"Oh, I heard about that! I can't remember their name, but apparently the lead singer is super dreamy." Dee said, wiggling her eyebrows. "I wish I could meet you there, but I have tickets to go see a play with my mom this weekend."

"That's too bad," Savanah replied with a pout. "But I'll let you know about the gorgeous lead singer."

"Deal!" Dee exclaimed with a dimpled smile as she met her friend's eyes and added, "And Savanah, promise me you'll let loose and have some fun."

* * *

AFTER A WONDERFUL SURPRISE and an even more amazing Dinner at the Blue Corn, Garrett, Bea, their friends Hayden and Whitney Hastings with their infant son, Bauer, and Bea's housemate Marnie Perez, all walked from the restaurant towards the park to take in the Main Stage concert. Savanah was grateful Marnie was joining them. Having met Marnie a few times through Bea, she instantly liked her and was grateful to have another single friend with their group. Savanah always found herself avoiding hanging out with couples, as she hated feeling like a third wheel.

Reaching the large community park, they found a nice spot to sit down on the grass with a good view of the stage, just as the sun was making its descent.

"Do you know who's playing tonight?" Savanah asked Marnie curiously, taking a seat next to her.

Marnie let out a little chuckle. "My brother's band, Prairie Sound." she replied excitedly. "I can't wait for you to hear them! Once it starts, maybe we can move closer?"

Savanah's eyes widened in surprise. *Marnie's brother's band. Could Marnie's brother be the dreamy lead singer?* Although being front and center wasn't Savanah's thing, she replied, "Ooh yes, let's do that. I'm so curious now!"

"He's single too, Savanah. Just saying." informed Bea with a coy wink.

"And he's hot," Whitney added with a playful wiggle of her brows.

"Hey, husband here!" Hayden exclaimed, feigning insult.

"Don't worry, baby, you are still the most handsome in all the land." Whitney reassured him, spreading her arms out with a flourish before offering him a reassuring hug and a pat on his chest.

Savanah giggled along with the others. She enjoyed Bea's friends and, looking at Hayden and Whitney, she admired the affection and love they had for each other. *Will I ever find that kind of love?*

The lights came up on the stage and the unmistakable sound of an electric guitar drifted over the open expanse of the park. A man appeared on stage, tight dark wash jeans, a black t-shirt that showed off muscular forearms, leather cuffs on his wrists, and black combat boots. Savanah could make out his dark features and lean, toned build. Even a distance away, she could see what Dee was talking about. *Wow, he is dreamy.*

Marnie sprang to her feet and put her hand out to Savanah. "Let's get up there so we can get a good spot."

Savanah took her hand and Marnie whisked her away from the others, weaving her between groups of people, towards the front of the stage. Satisfied with their proximity to the stage, she turned to Savanah and shouted over the sound of the guitar solo, "This is perfect."

Savanah's eyes darted around, taking in the scene. She had never been so close to the front of a concert stage and felt a little out of sorts at first, but glancing at Marnie, eyes pinned to the stage with excitement radiating off her, Savanah started to relax. Her gaze rose to the stage. The lead singer, now flagged by his three other bandmates, his eyes closed as he shredded the guitar. He opened his eyes, a rich chocolate brown and so beautiful and soulful, staring out at the crowd. *Somewhat familiar.* The singer glanced down, offering Marnie a smile, and slowly his gaze drifted over to Savanah. Recognition hit her like a freight train, and she blinked slowly, deliberately, hardly believing her own eyes. With disbelief, she stared up at the endearing lopsided smile of her camp crush, her first kiss, Ramiro Perez.

Rami grabbed the mic and started to belt out a rock classic, and Savanah knew that tone of voice immediately. It was deeper, more mature, but there was no mistaking it. Her Rami was up on that stage. Her heart beat faster at the realization and excitement consumed her at seeing him again. Now rather than a tall handsome teen boy she had a crush on that summer at Camp Clearwater, Rami was an impossibly sexy rockstar. His deep edgy voice cut through sharp as a razor and she stood there mesmerized, not able to take her eyes off him.

"Aren't they awesome?" Marnie shouted over the thundering beat of the music, the swell of the crowd and the thrumming of her heart.

Savanah was speechless. She just nodded, completely captivated by the gorgeous man in front of her. As he moved across the stage, she watched as he drew in the crowd, girls screaming, everyone dancing to the music. Realizing she was just standing there, dumbstruck and staring, she started swaying to the music along with the crowd. The entire experience was exhilarating. She had been to concerts before, but never one like this. Never the concert of someone she knew so well. Never the concert of someone who wrapped her up in the warmth of unforgettable memories and revisited her thoughts again and again over the past eight years. Someone she always wondered about and wished she could get in touch with.

The band played hit after hit, the crowd hungry for more and Rami giving them exactly what they craved. As the music slowed, switching gears to a slow set, Rami set his electric guitar aside and reached for an acoustic guitar as one of his bandmates behind a keyboard started to play. She recognized the hook immediately, and her eyes widened. It was her song, the one he sang for her at the camp talent show. Her favorite song. He sang the first line of "Sky Full of Stars" and Savanah thought she might melt into a puddle right there on the park lawn. She closed her eyes and took in the words, his deep sultry voice, so husky yet sweet.

"Isn't he super talented?" Marnie asked proudly, breaking her from her trance. "He sings this song at every concert he does. I once asked him why and all he said was that it's special to him."

Savanah turned to Marnie with an incredulous look on her face as she asked. "Every time?"

Marnie nodded, oblivious to the cacophony of emotions raging inside of Savanah as she continued. "He's never told me the story, but he just says it reminds him of someone he knew once."

Savanah glanced up at Rami and his melting chocolate gaze meet hers as a flood of memories of the night of that talent show and their sweet and tender kiss on the dock washed over her. As quickly as the memory resurfaced, sweet recognition swept over Rami's handsome face. His lips curved up in a knowing smile and as if no time had passed between them, Savanah's heart did a flip flop.

* * *

RAMI HAD FEW REGRETS. He approached life full steam ahead and seldom took the time to look back. However, now, here on this stage, performing a song that brought on the sweet memory of stars reflected in mesmerizing baby blues, the one regret that he couldn't shake was staring up at him. The beautiful blue eyes of Savanah Smithfield, his first camp friend, first crush and the girl he dreamt of ever since they'd kissed on that dock eight years ago. The girl he wished he gave his phone number to so they could keep in touch. The prettiest girl he had ever seen in his life was here in the front row, next to his sister. *How does she know Marnie?* Questions started running through his head as he sang, his eyes transfixed on her. *You're in the middle of a show*, he reminded himself, even though what he really wanted was to jump off the stage and wrap her in a huge hug.

The entire show Rami tried everything he could to stay focused on the songs and focused on the energy of the crowd, however the entire time, his eyes kept darting over to Savanah in the front row watching him, just to ensure she wasn't a figment of his imagination, or a mirage brought on by the summer heat and stage lights. He could tell his bandmates noticed flashing him knowing looks as they played and amused smiles in between songs. Rami had always been considered a bit of a ladies' man amongst them and had always been charming and flirty with their female fans, but he had never been completely shaken by a girl until tonight. *They're not going to let me live this one down.*

Their show finished with an encore, and the band gave one last wave to the crowd. Rami, as usual, lingering a bit longer, waving to their adoring fans, before finally exiting the stage.

Their drummer, Rex, turned to him and asked with a gruff laugh, "Dude, what was that? You had your eyes pinned to that pink bunny in the front all night."

"Don't call her a bunny." Rami said, squinting and giving him a side eye.

Rex held his hands up in surrender, still laughing and shaking his head. "She had you shaken, dude."

"She was definitely a beauty." Their bass player, Layne commented, letting out a low whistle.

"Seriously beautiful." Steve, their keyboardist, added. "She was with Marnie too. Are they friends or something?"

Before Rami could respond, Rex's eyes darted past him. "Incoming…" he said out of the corner of his mouth.

A group of giggling girls approached them, notebooks and pens in hand.

"Hello, ladies!" Rami greeted, flashing them his megawatt smile and a flirtatious wink. "Did you enjoy the show?"

The girls gushed and giggled as Rami charmed every one of them, his bandmates following his lead. With selfies and autographs in hand, they drifted off, and he glanced around, spotting her immediately, a vision with flowing pink hair, next to his sister Marnie. *My Savanah.* Their eyes met and like a magnet to metal, he found himself pulled towards her. *Does she even remember me?* A voice of doubt echoed in his head as he sauntered over, his bandmates hanging back and watching him with interest. *Be cool.* An unexpected nervousness rose in his chest as Marnie beamed and as Savanah turned, her eyes meeting his, an endearingly shy smile curled her lips.

"You were amazing tonight!" Marnie exclaimed proudly, as she wrapped an arm around him and turned to Savanah. "Rami, this is my friend, Savanah Smithfield. Savanah, this is my brother, Rami Perez."

It is her. He offered her a nostalgic smile, and her beautiful eyes shone back with recognition. "Hi Savanah. It's so amazing to see you again," he rasped, nervously going in for a hug.

"Rami, I thought that was you." she replied with a sweet giggle as she hugged him back, the feel of her warm, lean body, the soft brush of her silky hair against his cheek and sweet smell of her rose scented perfume jumbling his thoughts. She released their embrace and stared up at him, her blue eyes dancing as she added, "Except now you're a rockstar!"

Uncharacteristically, his cheeks flushed a little as he waved his hand in the air, brushing off the compliment. "I'm still the same guy you knew back at Camp Clearwater. Except a little taller and a little older."

Savanah graced him with an affectionate smile, and he couldn't help but take in the stunning woman in front of him. She had undoubtedly changed. She too was a little taller, almost six foot he estimated, slender but more curvaceous than he remembered. The lines of her face, more contoured and mature. Her face was still the prettiest he had ever seen, with gorgeous big blue eyes, long dark thick lashes, freckles on her perfectly arched nose and beautiful pink pillowy lips. Soft lips he could still feel when he closed his eyes and thought of their kiss.

"You two know each other?" Marnie asked, her eyebrows raised in surprise, breaking Rami from his thoughts. "Camp Clearwater?"

"Ah, yeah, Savanah and I were close friends for about five years until our last summer at camp, like, eight years ago." Rami explained, glancing over to Savanah as she nodded in concurrence.

Marnie glanced between them, Rami knowing she was

combing her memory bank as her eyes brightened and she said, "Savanah, yes, I think I remember you talking about her. Wasn't it a Savanah that you had your first kiss with?"

Savanah held her hand up with a slight blush blooming on her cheeks. "That was me."

Marnie let out an incredulous laugh. "What a small world." She said with a wide smile. "You were all he could talk about after that summer."

"It was a memorable night." Rami added, locking his eyes on Savanah's sparkling gaze.

"It was," she whispered under her breath, clasping her hands in front of her and rocking on her heels.

"What are you both doing now? Do you have plans?" Rami asked, selfishly not wanting to let Savanah out of his sight.

"I was going to find Bea and Garrett and head back with them." Marnie answered, letting out a yawn. "Bakery hours have turned me into an old lady on the weekend."

Rami turned his gaze to Savanah, who replied. "I was going to check out the fair downtown."

"Would you like some company?" Rami asked eagerly, then turned to his band, who were still watching from a distance away. "My bandmates, Rex, Layne and Steve, want to head to the beer garden, but I'm not too keen on drinking tonight. I would rather hang out with you, if you want some company."

"Sure. We can catch up." Savanah answered softly with a shy smile.

Marnie glanced from Rami to Savanah and back again,

a knowing look on her face. "Okay, there little brother, take care of Savanah."

"She's safe with me," Rami said, saluting his sister and letting his gaze drift back to Savanah.

Marnie rolled her eyes, gave them both a quick hug and strode off, texting Bea as she went.

Savanah looked up at Rami, her eyes twinkling as she asked. "So which direction?"

Rami pointed towards the crowd slowly exiting the concert and likely headed towards the downtown area. Both strolled across the park lawn in contemplative silence, taking to the sidewalk until they stopped at a crosswalk and Rami asked curiously. "So, how do you know my sister?"

"Her previous housemate, Bea, is marrying my brother, Garrett." Savanah answered. "So, I met Marnie through Bea. We became quick friends, and she also comes into my shop from time to time."

"Shop? What kind of shop?" Rami asked with interest, as the light turned green for them to cross.

"I own a clothing boutique just a block from here called Pretty Things." Savanah answered with a proud smile. "I sell unique clothes, shoes, and accessories."

"Wow, what made you want to open your own boutique?"

"I modeled for almost five years and really fell in love with fashion," she shared as they strolled down the side-walk. "But I didn't enjoy the modeling scene. Too much partying, unrealistic expectations on the models to main-tain themselves, that kind of stuff. It wasn't me," she continued. "So, I went to business school and opened my boutique. My mission is for every woman or girl that walks into my store to find something that makes them feel pretty and special."

Rami offered her his lopsided smile as he asked, "So, empowerment is your thing?"

Savanah nodded and let out a little giggle. "Exactly."

"That's truly amazing, Savanah." Rami complimented. "I mean, to be so young, and to have accomplished so much, is something to be seriously proud of."

"Thanks." Savanah humbly replied, flipping the tables on him. "How about you? I mean, I remember you telling me you were going to start a band with some friends, but look at you now!"

"Yep, a rockstar wannabe," he said, offering her a self-deprecating smirk.

"You are a rockstar, Rami. You commanded that stage tonight!" Savanah exclaimed, nudging his arm playfully. "I couldn't take my eyes off you, and you were..." Savanah glanced away, a rosy hue creeping up her cheeks as she finished her thoughts. "You were amazing."

Rami grinned, teasingly volleying a question. "You couldn't keep your eyes off me? What if I told you I couldn't keep my eyes off you?"

Savanah stopped walking, gazed up at him and cocked her eyebrow at him, a smile curving her lips.

"You're still as pretty as I remember." Rami went on as he confessed. "I had the hugest crush on you, and I still think of that night on the dock."

"I think of it too." Savanah admitted, her eyes drawing him in and ensnaring them in their hold. "I had a crush on you, too. I mean, you were pretty much the reason I kept going back to camp every year."

"So, tell me why, then, didn't we exchange phone numbers?" Rami asked.

"Not sure," she replied with a wistful shrug as they continued slowly down the sidewalk. "I've thought about that many times over the years. Perhaps there was a magic about only meeting up at camp each summer." She mused, a nostalgic smile tugging at her lips. "I know it felt that way for me."

Rami reflected on that for a moment and smiled. "Magic. I like that."

As they reached the part of main street that was blocked off for the fair, the sound of the midway and music greeted them. Delicious smells from the food vendors wafted through the air, tempting fair goers to stop and buy their favorite treats.

"Would you like some popcorn or cotton candy?" Savanah asked. "I can't attend the fair without getting some cotton candy."

"Popcorn, but it's my treat." Rami insisted, getting into line and pulling out his wallet.

Savanah gave him a gracious smile as he ordered a box of popcorn, and a bundle of pink cotton candy, then paid the vendor.

"Thank you." Savanah said as he handed her the bag of cotton candy and they leisurely strolled through the crowd. They made their way past carnival games and vendors, stopping at a few to check them out as they continued down the main street towards the rides.

"Do you like Ferris wheels?" Rami asked, glancing up at the brightly lit wheel in front of them.

"Never been on one." Savanah replied, shrugging her shoulders and glancing up at the ride. "So, I don't know."

"Well, then today is your lucky day," he said, grabbing her hand and leading her over to the closest ticket booth.

* * *

SAVANAH LOOKED DOWN at her hand in his as they waited for ride tickets. Rami made no move to let go, and she wasn't about to pull away. Something about the warmth of his hand and fingers laced with hers felt comfortable and familiar and she marveled at how something as simple as hand holding felt so good.

"Come with me," he said, showing her the tickets in his hand as he guided her through the crowd to the lineup for the Ferris wheel.

A girl shouted from the lineup, "Hey that's the singer from Prairie Sound." and dozens of people turned their heads towards them. Rami nodded graciously with a smile and a wave, acknowledging the fan but never let go of Savanah's hand. Their turn came, and they took their seats, sliding in next to each other. Savanah's pulse quickened from their proximity as she caught his scent. A subtle mix of sandalwood cologne and sweat so masculine and enticing it made her head spin.

Rami glanced down at where he held her hand and smiled hesitantly, letting go. "Sorry, I hadn't realized I was still holding your hand."

Savanah immediately felt the loss of warmth but met

his chocolate brown eyes. "That's okay," she replied, folding her hands on her lap as the carnival worker locked the bar across their seats. The metal seat rocked back a little and creaked as the wheel started to move. Savanah's eyes widened as she looked at the ground disappearing beneath them, her heart racing as she flashed Rami a trepidatious look.

"Are you scared?" Rami asked, his brows drawing together in concern.

"A little." Savanah replied honestly, surveying the seat and the bar that locked them in. "Heights have never really been my thing."

"I promise it'll be fine," he said, putting his arm around her and pulling her closer. "I got you."

As the wheel climbed to the top, the entire scope of the fair came into view. The lights, the sounds of the midway, the colorful carnival games, the people milling about, the lineups, the music. It was sensory overload in the best possible way, and yet, from up high, you felt like you were in your own little world. Savanah looked out at the scene below them and Rami gave her shoulder a squeeze.

"We can see everything from up here. Awesome, right?"

Savanah nodded, feeling warm and cozy pressed up to him. She plucked a piece of her cotton candy from the bag and popped it into her mouth, letting the sugary confection melt on her tongue as she sighed contentedly.

"Comfy?" Rami asked, the side of his mouth tilting up into his signature smirk.

"This is nice," she answered happily. "I don't go out much as I work a lot. Honestly, I'm a bit of an introvert, so this evening has been great." She confessed, looking up and meeting his brown eyes reflecting the colorful midway lights.

He reached over and touched the side of her face gently, the gesture making her pulse quicken instantly. "You are so beautiful, Savanah." he complimented with saccharine sincerity dripping from his voice. "Can I kiss you?"

A pleasant sense of déjà vu washed over her as Savanah flashed back to their first kiss on the dock, the same combination of nervousness and excitement fluttering in her belly as she took in his question. Her tongue darted out, instinctively moistening her bottom lip and Rami's eyes followed, then rose back up to meet her gaze. "Yes." she replied on a breath. "You can kiss me."

Rami lifted her chin, his soulful chocolate eyes transfixed on hers, a serene look on his face. He lowered his lips to hers, brushing them softly and sweetly, not making a move to deepen the kiss but not leaving her to question his interest in her. His kiss was so tender it made all her emotions from eight years ago resurface and her body melted into him. His lips leaving hers, she opened her eyes, his endearing smile greeting her. She smiled back and laid her head against his shoulder, letting out a big sigh as he pulled her in for a hug.

"This has been an amazing night. Can we do it again?"

Savanah's eyes darted up to meet Rami as a little giggle escaped. "Well, I guess you'll need my phone number then."

* * *

Savanah entered her boutique with her favorite coffee in hand. Flicking on lights as she went, illuminating her shop. She set her coffee down on the front counter and combed the racks as she always did, ensuring everything was hung properly and displays were in order. A knock at the front window made her turn, and she saw Dee's shining face smiling at her through the glass. Her best friend was a recent graduate of Education and although she was taking on substitute teaching jobs, she was also Savanah's main employee at Pretty Things.

"Good morning, Dee!" Savanah greeted, unlocking the front door to let her in. "How was your weekend?"

"Oh, good, the play was ah-mazing!" she replied with a bright dimpled smile before she placed a hand on her hip and ensnared Savanah with a questioning look. "But girl, I don't want to talk about me. I think you had a better weekend than I did!" she exclaimed, producing a newspaper she had tucked under her arm. Placing it on the counter, she opened it and pointed at a picture on the front page.

Savanah looked at where she was pointing to see a picture of her and Rami kissing on the Ferris wheel. Savanah's face took on a rosy hue as she read the caption. *"Love at the Fair."*

"Spill, girl!" Dee urged, cocking a curious brow at Savanah.

Savanah could feel the heat settle in her cheeks, and she smiled, thinking about how amazing it felt to have Rami's arm wrapped around her. She let out a long breath as she explained, "So, you know that band I was going to see, Prairie Sound?" Savanah began. Dee nodded, her eyes brightening as she leaned over the counter, eager to know the scoop. "Well, the lead singer is my Camp Clearwater crush."

"The one you had your first kiss with?" Dee asked, her eyes widening, remembering Savanah sharing the story with her so many years ago.

"Yes, Ramiro Perez, my one and only camp crush and the dreamy lead singer of Prairie Sound are one and the same." Dee clapped gleefully, her entire attention enrapt. "We reconnected after the concert. His sister is Marnie Perez. You know Bea's friend, who comes in here with her sometimes."

"Yeah, Bea's old housemate." Dee remembered as she rolled her hand, gesturing for her to go on.

"Yes, well, afterwards Marnie had to head home, and I was going to check out the fair, so Rami asked if he could join me. And well, long story short, we had an amazing time, shared a kiss on the Ferris wheel and exchanged phone numbers." Savanah concluded with a long exhale as she touched her hands to her warm blushing face and continued in a rush of words. "Honesty, Dee, I was so shocked to see him again and he was just so incredible on that stage. I was in complete awe watching him perform. He's so talented and crazy charismatic! Then we talked, and it was like not a day had passed. It was like talking to my old friend."

"But now a super sexy rockstar." Dee added with a wink.

Savanah let out a dreamy sigh. "So sexy."

Dee laughed and patted Savanah on the back. "You need a little sexy in your life, my friend. Something to shake things up a little for you. Perhaps a hot and sexy rockstar is just what the doctor ordered."

Savanah thought about Dee's words. She had become stagnant when it came to love in her life. She was just taking things day by day and living a very calm and quiet existence. *Am I ready for a shakeup?* Glancing down at the picture of them again, her heart warming and her lips tingling at the memory of that kiss, she knew her answer. *Yes, I am!*

CHAPTER 2

*R*ami couldn't get Savanah out of his head. It had been three days since the concert in the park. Three days since they were reunited, and three days since he kissed her on the Ferris wheel. Three days he waited to call her in an attempt to not come across too eager. The truth was, he was eager. He wanted to see her. To stare into those beautiful blue eyes, feel the warmth of her body pressed to his, and to smell her intoxicating sweet and floral scent. Just being in her orbit threw his mind and heart into a tailspin, and that whirling feeling was addictive.

It's not that he lacked options in the love department. He met women all the time. Many threw themselves at him. Some women were so forward, slipping their digits in his pockets and fawning all over him. Pawing at him even when he didn't want to be touched. He wasn't interested in that. Despite his flirtatious ladies' man and rocker persona, he wanted the real deal, and Savanah Smithfield, although breathtakingly gorgeous, was the real deal.

He pulled out his phone and found her phone number. Glancing at the clock, he wondered if it was too late to call, but quickly cast his questions aside, selecting her number, and hitting the call symbol. He drummed his fingers on the countertop as his phone connected.

"Hello!" her soft voice answered.

Damn, her voice is sweet. "Hi Savanah. It's Rami." he said. "Am I catching you at a bad time?"

"No, not at all." She replied, the genuine happiness in her voice his assurance. "I'm just curled up on the couch with a book."

"What are you reading?" he asked curiously.

"Just a romance novel."

"So, you like romance novels?" he asked mentally, storing this information away. "I assume you love romantic movies as well?"

"Of course." She replied, her tone almost wistful as she added. "If you don't have romance in your life, at least you can watch, or in my case tonight, read about it."

Rami thought about her words for a moment. *Savanah was lacking romance in her life. How could someone so beautiful inside and out not have romance in her life?*

"I personally think you deserve all the romance." Rami replied with sincerity.

Savanah let out a nervous giggle as she responded, "I know I do, but..."

"But, what?" Rami pressed.

"I don't exactly get asked out very often and then when someone finally does ask me out, they seem to focus on my appearance. They never even try to get to know my personality or what's in my heart." She shared with an exasperated sigh.

"You want them to know that you're more than a pretty face."

"Exactly." she replied in a resigned tone. "I hope that doesn't come across as vain."

Savanah was unmistakably a knockout, but she was so much more than that. Her kindness and sweetness radiated from within. "Not at all," he replied with deep sincerity. "There's absolutely nothing vain about you." A moment of awkward silence fell on them both. Rami was almost able to feel her shy smile through the phone at his compliment. *Ask her, ask her!* Rami's internal voice chanted. "Savanah, would you like to go out with me tomorrow night?" he asked, his question coming out in a nervous rush. "I...I would like to get to know you again and spend some time with you."

"I would really like that, Rami." she replied. "What did you have in mind?"

They made plans to meet, and Rami hung up his phone, his head reeling, a plan formulating in his mind. *Savanah deserves to be valued for more than her pretty face. She needs to be pursued and romanced and I'm going to be the guy to do it.* Determination filled his chest and a million ideas rushed through his head. *I need to recruit help and I know exactly who to talk to.*

* * *

SAVANAH SURVEYED the parking lot and glanced at her phone, double checking the address Rami texted her. He had given her this address to meet him, but as she looked up at the sign on the building, Twinkle Toes Dance Academy, she wondered if she was in the wrong place. Savanah smoothed down her pink and white striped sundress, suddenly second guessing her choice of outfit for this date, her first with Rami.

"Hey there." A deep voice sounded behind her, and she turned around to be greeted by Rami's twinkling brown eyes and handsome smile. His eyes drifted over her with approval. "You look gorgeous."

"Thank you." she beamed, her doubt on her outfit all but forgotten with his compliment. "You look pretty good yourself." she added, perusing his attire.

He was dressed in a short sleeve black button-down shirt, slim fit dark wash jeans and his black combat boots. The shirt had the top two buttons open, giving her a tease of his smooth, toned chest, which she had to admit was very sexy.

"Thank you," he said, holding up a large paper takeout bag. The bag said Ling Family Chinese Restaurant.

Her eyes widened with surprise as she asked, "How did you know? Chinese food is my favorite!"

"I have my ways," he answered, giving her a playful wink and with a deep chuckle, looked up at the sign on the building. "Are you wondering why we're here?"

"Yes!" she exclaimed with a giggle. "Twinkle Toes Dance Academy?"

"My cousin teaches here. Come with me," he replied, opening the door, and letting her enter first. The sound of kids giggling and music coming from a studio made Savanah smile. She had taken dance classes as a kid and the memory for her was a fond one. A beautiful dark-haired woman Savanah guessed to be in her early thirties greeted them with a warm smile. Rami introduced her as his cousin and the woman leaned in, saying something quietly to him in Spanish. Rami thanked her graciously, and he took Savanah's hand, leading her to a studio near the back of the dance academy. They entered a darkened space and Rami flicked on the lights. The room illuminated with strings of fairy lights draped from the ceiling. Savanah's breath caught at the sight, the lights reflecting on the shiny wood dance floor and mirrors making the entire studio shimmer and sparkle. In the middle of the dance floor was a picnic blanket, along with large, cozy pillows.

"Rami, this is beautiful." Savanah marveled, turning around, taking in the perimeter of the room. He gave her his handsome smile and reached for her hand, feathering his fingers with hers, leading her over to the picnic set up. Taking a seat and slipping off her ballet flats to get comfortable, she curled her long legs under her and straightened out her skirt, finding a comfortable position.

He sat down next to her and opened the takeout bag. He handed her a La Croix, her drink of choice, and proceeded to take out carton after carton of heavenly smelling Chinese food. Opening each one, she checked out his selections, marveling at how he got all her favorites. He handed her a plate and held up a fork and a pair of chopsticks. "Which do you prefer?" She grabbed the chopsticks, and he gave her a nod of approval. "I've never been able to master those," he said, a fork in hand gesturing for her to dig in.

"I spent a little time in Asia when I was modeling and got pretty proficient," she replied, putting a little of everything on her plate using her chopsticks.

"Asia? Where did you all travel to?" he asked curiously.

"All over Canada, the United States, Europe and once to Asia for an editorial photo shoot." she replied. "I only modeled for five years, but I got the opportunity to see some really amazing places."

"That's great that you got to travel. I hope Prairie Sound will eventually be signed and get picked up by a big tour," he shared between bites. "I dream of traveling one day."

"So, that's the goal. Record, and tour?" she asked.

"That's the plan. I don't want to be a cover band anymore, though. I want us to play and record our own original songs. My bandmates are on board with that too."

"Does that mean you won't be singing my song anymore?" she asked, playfully giving him a nudge.

"Anytime you want me to sing that song, you just have to ask," he replied with a wink.

They continued their picnic, laughing and talking about work, his band, and their families, with conversation coming easily and abundantly. When they were done eating, he gathered up the leftovers and tucked them back into the bag, cleaning up the space. Savanah watched as Rami walked over to the sound system in the corner and put a CD in the player, glancing over at her with a look of mischief on his face. He pressed play and "(I've Had) The Time of my Life", the theme from *Dirty Dancing,* drifted from the speakers. He walked over to her slowly, putting his hand out to her. "May I have this dance?"

Savanah looked up at him, feeling all fluttery as she took his hand. He pulled her up to her feet, bringing her flush with his hard, lean body, and she looked up at him shyly through her long lashes. He smiled, turning her, his front to her back. Her breath hitched as he curled her arm up around the back of his neck and he caressed the back of his hand down the inside of her arm, grazing over the side of her body, making her shiver and goosebumps form on her skin. He grabbed her hand and spun her out making her skirt lift with the momentum. She let out a giggle, and he laughed too as he brought her back against him, gripping her waist as he ground his hips on her thighs. "Are you trying to dirty dance with me?" she giggled at his rather sexy attempt to reenact the Patrick Swayze moves from one of her favorite romantic movies.

"Attempting may be the right description," he replied with a wink, and she rocked her hips to match his rhythm. "Nice moves," he said, his eyes flashing playfully. He spun her around a few times then let her go as the breakdown of the song started and he gave a rather impressive pause and grind just like Patrick Swayze did in the movie before he strutted away from her glancing over his shoulder once giving her a smoldering sexy look. Turning around fully and clapping his hands together, he exclaimed, "Run to me, I'm ready for you!"

Savanah gave him a look like he had lost his mind and asked. "You want to lift me like in the movie?"

"Yep, I lug around equipment to shows and these guns can without question lift a lightweight like you," he said flexing his rather impressive biceps.

Savanah had to admit he looked strong, like he could

lift her if he wanted to. Pushing aside her apprehension, she surveyed Rami across the room, looking so impossibly handsome and ready to catch her. Deciding to trust him, she backed up and ran towards him at full speed. When she reached him, he grabbed her by the waist and lifted her high in the air. She pointed her arms out in front of her, and her toes out behind her trying to even out her weight, creating a balance. He held her for a moment and laughed as he brought her down from the lift slowly, her body sliding down the length of his, making her breathless from both the adrenaline and his proximity. He let out a big exhale and smiled as he gripped her waist, their faces just inches from each other.

"How's that for romance?" he whispered, his eyes sparkling from the twinkle of the fairy lights.

"Epic." she replied, her eyes transfixed on his dreamy gaze.

"This is just the beginning." He promised, reaching up and caressing her cheek. She closed her eyes, savoring the gentleness of his touch on her face. The heat of his breath hovered over her mouth so close it made her head spin. Finally, he brushed his soft lips to hers, making her melt in his arms. The kiss was sweet and reverent, making her yearn for more, but appreciative of his restraint. His lips left hers and he pulled her in for a hug, her arms wrapping around his trim waist. They stood there a long time, both swaying, no music but the sound of their hearts drumming steadily in their chests. Savanah looked up at the ceiling, the fairy lights twinkling, reminding her of the stars in the night sky. "You know, those lights up there look like stars," she said, meeting his tender gaze. "Can you sing me my song?"

He smiled as he began to sing the smooth tone of his voice enveloping her like the best hug. Savanah sighed and settled her head on his shoulder, thinking she could stay like this forever.

CHAPTER 3

Rami was floating. Buoyant and light, each step taking on a giddy bounce. Last night had been everything he hoped it would be, and more. The plan to reenact one of Savanah's favorite romantic movies was perfect and he could tell by her affection towards him and how she melted in his arms, that she appreciated it too. His mission to romance Savanah was off to a great start, and date number two was already brewing in his head.

"Earth to Rami." Layne said with a deep chuckle. "Where'd you go there?"

"Sorry." Rami apologized, picking up his guitar and shaking his head, trying to clear the blissful fog. "I was daydreaming."

"Thinking about the pink bunny again?" Rex asked with a snicker and a waggle of his eyebrows.

Rami narrowed his eyes at Rex as he replied, "Her name is Savanah, and yes, we had a date last night. I seriously can't get her out of my head," he confessed, grabbing a stool from the corner of Layne's garage, and taking a seat. "I don't think I've told you guys this, but Savanah and I were friends a long time ago. We met at summer camp when we were just kids."

"Hey, I remember you telling me this story. Is she the reason you always add that Coldplay song to our playlist?" Layne queried, a slow smile curling his lips.

Rami nodded, a flashback of nostalgia washing over his features as he grinned at his bandmates and replied, "It's her favorite song."

Steve took his place behind his keyboard, flipping it on and pressing down a key as he asked, glancing up to Rami, his eyes shining with his question, "This Savanah is the real deal, then?"

"She is." Rami answered, running his hand over his face, his eyes flitting between his friends. "Savanah's not like the girls we tend to meet when gigging. She's different. She's special."

"The ladies' man is off the market." Layne declared, offering him a smile and clapping him on the back. "Good on you, man."

"It's about time! More chicks for me." Rex answered with a big, cheesy grin before he furrowed his brows and picked up his drumsticks. "Okay, enough of this lovey dovey bull shit. What you got for us today, Romeo?"

Rami shook his head and let out a conceding laugh as he reached for his guitar and replied, "I got a killer idea for a song."

* * *

SAVANAH WALKED down the main street of Primrose with Amelia's hand in hers listening as she regaled her with stories about her friends and her first year living in Primrose. Today was a gorgeous August evening, with a light breeze keeping the relentless heat of summer bearable. A perfect evening for a stroll with her beloved niece. Savanah loved being an aunt and any time she had to spend with Amelia was time she looked forward to and cherished.

"Aunty Savanah, can we stop at the bakery and get a treat?" Amelia asked, as she tugged at her arm and stared up at her with her big blue eyes.

Savanah glanced up to see the sign Everything You Knead boldly displayed across the top of the building. She had never been to Marnie's Bakery before, and since she would never turn down a sweet treat, her answer was simple. "Absolutely! Let's see what they have."

Pushing the door open, the chime sounded, and Savanah let Amelia walk inside first.

"Amelia!" a familiar deep voice exclaimed from across the counter. *Rami.* "Don't you look pretty today," he commented, flashing her a sweet smile.

Amelia struck a pose, showing off her cotton sundress with pink flowers on it. A big, bountiful laugh rumbled from his chest as his eyes drifted up to meet Savanah's, then boldly roamed over her flowy pink tank top that offered just a peak of midriff and cutoff jean shorts that accentuated the expanse of her long-tanned legs.

"A pair of pink princesses," he added, his voice edging on husky, as their gazes met, affection reflecting back at her. "Hi Savanah."

A warm rush enveloped her body, liking the way he looked at her as she remembered their date, his strong arms holding her to him as they swayed gently, and he sang her song under dozens of twinkling fairy lights. They had been texting every day for the past two weeks, but had both been too busy to connect on the phone or in person.

"Hi Rami. I had no idea you worked here." She said, glancing around Marnie's quaint bakery. *Adorable.*

"I help Marnie when she needs me. I'm usually here a few times a week." He replied, his gorgeous eyes never leaving hers as he leaned over the counter looking like her every dream.

"Lucky us," Savanah answered, a hint of flirtation in her comment.

"Lucky me," he volleyed back, a smile slowly curving on his lips as his eyes returned to Amelia. "Let me guess, you're here for a cupcake?"

"Yes!" Amelia replied, looking into the showcase and spotting the last two pink cupcakes available.

"Would you like one?" Rami asked, meeting Savanah's gaze with a delighted twinkle. "I got two."

"Sure. They look amazing!" Savanah replied, taking in the vanilla cupcake piled high with pink frosting and a big juicy strawberry on top.

Rami pulled both cupcakes out of the showcase and plated them before handing them over. Amelia carefully carried hers to a table, making herself comfortable.

Savanah pulled out her wallet and Rami waved her off. "No charge."

She tilted her head and gave him a chiding look. "You don't need to do that. I'm happy to pay."

"We're closing in 30 minutes, and you're doing me a favor. Less for me to take home and eat," he replied, with a laugh as he patted his trim stomach.

Savanah offered him a look of thanks as she made her way to the table where Amelia was seated and slid into the seat next to her. Amelia had already plucked the strawberry off her cupcake, her mouth full of the juicy berry.

Rami disappeared into the back kitchen and reappeared a minute later holding two glasses of ice water and gestured to the seat across from them. "May I join you lovely ladies?"

Both Savanah and Amelia nodded, and he took a seat. Savanah plucked the strawberry from her cupcake, scooping up some of the pink frosting before bringing it to her lips to take a bite. Rami's eyes followed her movement and flickered with mirth as he leaned back casually and put his arm around the back of the chair next to him. "So, I have a question for you, Savanah. Something I've been wondering since we reconnected." He explained, cocking his head slightly as his eyes danced playfully.

"Ask away." She replied, tearing a piece of the cupcake off and popping it into her mouth.

"Why pink hair?" he asked, a smile curving his lips. "I mean, I love it and honestly, I think it looks fantastic on you, but I've been wondering why pink? Note, my bandmate Rex has a blue mohawk and I'm all for self-expression."

Savanah sat back, her blue eyes gleaming at his question as she answered, "Obviously I like pink…" she started pointing to her flowy tank top.

"I like pink too!" Amelia exclaimed, pink icing on the tip of her nose.

Both Rami and Savanah laughed as Rami got up from his seat and retrieved a few napkins from the counter, handing them to Amelia.

"…And at first dying my hair pink was a rebellious thing for me." Savanah explained, picking at the cupcake liner. "When I got out of modeling and away from a world where everyone told me what to wear and what I should look like, I wanted to do something unexpected."

"I assume rebellion isn't your usual MO then?" he clarified, the side of his mouth tilting up into his handsome smirk.

"Not at all. I'm pretty boring, actually." She replied with a shrug and a nervous giggle.

Rami leaned forward, stretching his arm across the table and reaching for her hand. "Savanah, you're anything but boring," he said, his eyes gleaming back at her.

Savanah's heart did that familiar flip-flop, and she gave him a shy smile, as she popped another bite of the cupcake in her mouth and shook her head pointing to the remaining cupcake on her plate as she chewed and mumbled, holding her hand to her mouth. "These are seriously amazing. Probably the best cupcake I've ever had."

"Marnie is a brilliant baker," he declared proudly of his sister. "Did I tell you I live with her?"

"Right across the street from Garrett and Bea?" Savanah asked, before taking another bite of her cupcake.

He nodded and glanced up at the clock on the wall. "It's almost closing time, so if you hang tight, I can walk back with you two."

"We'd like that."

Rami got up from the table and Savanah brought her attention to Amelia. As Rami went about his closing routine, she couldn't help but steal glances at him. Rami was lean and tall, all dark features and tanned skin. *It should be illegal to be that handsome.* Rami caught her gaze several times, flashing her his endearing smirk and making her heart beat faster with each one. Once all cleaning was done, he disappeared into the back and returned a few minutes later with a box of leftover goodies and a leather messenger bag slung over his lean frame.

"Ready to go?" he asked, glancing down at Amelia, then back to Savanah, meeting her gaze. She nodded, and he gestured for them to exit ahead of him so he could lock the door. Strolling together down the sidewalk, Amelia skipped ahead of them as Rami reached for Savanah's hand, threading his fingers with hers. The gesture was so natural and sweet it made Savanah smile. They crossed the main street and turned towards their destination when he spoke. "I was wondering what you're doing on Friday. I have band practice in the morning but have the rest of the day free. Do you think you could get off work early? Maybe around 3 p.m.? I can pick you up from your shop."

"I think I can make that work. I'm not sure you could

top our last date, though." She giggled, meeting his gaze with a playful grin. "Those were some pretty slick dance moves."

Rami straightened his back and puffed out his chest as he strutted along the sidewalk like John Travolta in "Saturday Night Fever". "I was proud of those moves. I watched that scene from the movie like twenty times to get that right."

"You went to all that trouble for me?" she asked, stopping and turning to face him, her eyes twinkling with mirth.

"Yes, and I would do it all over again," he said, coming closer and wrapping an arm around her waist, pulling her into him. "You deserve to be romanced, Savanah, so consider me the romance guru," he said, waggling his eyebrows at her.

Savanah giggled, looped her arms around his neck and threaded her fingers into the curls at the nape of his neck. "You're too cute," she said before pulling him in for a chaste kiss. "Looking forward to what you've planned for me next."

* * *

Savanah paced the length of her shop, stopping every now and then to take in her reflection in a shop mirror and straighten out her necklace or smooth down her ponytail. Rami had texted her the night before, telling her to dress casually but otherwise the romantic date he'd planned was a complete mystery.

"You're going to wear out that floor." Dee commented

with a raspy laugh. "I honestly have never seen you so anxious."

"Sorry, I'm just excited." She said, stopping at the front counter and fidgeting with her outfit. "Do I look okay?"

Dee gave her an appraising look, taking in her black skinny ankle length jeans, simple white V neck T-shirt, long slouchy rose-pink cardigan, and comfortable slip on pink and white sneakers. She wore her pink hair up in a slick ponytail and accessorized her outfit with a simple gold necklace and delicate dangly earrings.

"Seriously, Savanah, do you even have to ask?" Dee questioned with a roll of her eyes and a dismissive wave of her hand. "You always look effortless and gorgeous. Do you know what you're doing tonight?"

"No, idea. All he said was it was going to be romantic." She replied with a dreamy sigh.

Dee's face brightened, and she was about to comment further when the door chimes to the shop sounded and Rami, looking like a hot as sin rockstar walked in. He wore black skinny jeans ripped in all the right places displaying the tanned skin underneath, a white T-shirt that hugged his long lean frame to perfection and a long sleeve light blue jean button-down shirt worn open with the sleeves rolled up to his elbows showing off his muscular forearms. His black combat boots, brown leather cuffs on each wrist and dark sunglasses finished off his outfit.

"Well, hot damn." Dee declared under her breath so only Savanah could hear her.

Savanah's mouth went dry at the sight of him, and Dee gave her a nudge, breaking her from her trance. Rami approached the counter, removed his sunglasses and flashed them both his sexy smile before his gorgeous brown eyes caught Savanah in their crosshairs and he gave her a wink.

"Ladies." he said, his rich voice dripping with confidence and charisma as he zoned in on Dee, flashed her his megawatt smile and put out his hand to her. "Hi, I'm Rami Perez. You must be the famous best friend, Dee Jones."

Dee, nearly as entranced as Savanah, accepted his hand, a huge smile on her face and her dimples popping as she replied. "Nice to meet you, Rami. I don't know what Savanah told you about me, but it is all true." She drawled with a mischievous twinkle in her eye. "I am that amazing!"

One thing Savanah admired about her best friend was her confidence, which Dee had in spades.

Rami threw his head back in a deep bountiful laugh and returned his gaze to Savanah, his eyes drifting over her with appreciation as he put his arms out to her. Savanah bridged the gap between them, wrapping her arms around his taut waist. He smelled like mint and sandalwood, making her senses tingle as he lifted her chin and leaned down to tenderly brush his lips to hers.

Dee gave them both an approving smile and sighed. "You two crazy kids, have fun tonight." She said, waving them off towards the door.

Rami took Savanah's hand, his fingers intertwined with hers, and held the door open for her to walk through. They walked hand in hand down the sidewalk until they stopped in front of a sporty red Mazda RX-7 GT. "This is me," Rami said, opening the door for her.

Savanah dipped low and slipped inside as Rami came around the car, getting into the driver's side. The interior was black, nicely polished, and smelled like cinnamon from the air freshener dangling from the rear-view mirror. Savanah looked around and gave Rami a look of appreciation. "I like your car. It suits you. Kind of retro but sleek and sexy," she commented, smoothing her hand over the shiny dashboard.

"You think I'm sexy?" he teased; a coy eyebrow raised in question.

A blush settled on her cheeks at his question, and she rolled her eyes with a giggle. "You must know you have an effect on women."

He leaned over the console, his lips so close to hers she could almost taste them, as he searched her gaze. "You, Savanah, are the only woman that matters to me," he declared, capturing her lips in a sweet, chaste kiss. "Are you ready to be romanced, mi novia?" he asked, throwing a little Spanish her way and offering her a sexy grin.

Savanah giggled, wiggled her eyebrows, and replied. "Show me what you got Romance Guru!"

THEY DROVE for about an hour toward downtown Winnipeg. With St. Augustine and Primrose not far from the capital city, it made it easy to visit and check out the sights. Rami pulled into the parking lot across from the Manitoba Museum and Planetarium. Savanah's eyes flitted to Rami with a look of surprise on her face. "Is this our destination?"

"It sure is!" he replied, as he climbed out of the car, rounded the front of the vehicle and opened her door, offering her his hand. Savanah accepted as he helped her exit the car. Fingers laced together, he led her up the steps to the door of the museum and they slipped inside. Entering the lobby, he paid for their admissions for both the museum and a planetarium show and, hand in hand, they made their way into the gallery.

"I don't think I've been here since a 5th grade field trip." Savanah commented, taking in the displays as they leisurely strolled through the different galleries.

"This was always one of my favorite places to visit and one gallery in particular I always found super cool," he said, leading her down a dark narrow corridor towards a large dimly lit room.

Savanah remembered this gallery immediately as the grand replica of the merchant ship, the Nonsuch, came into view. As they stepped into the gallery, it felt like they were brought back in time to an old wharf town with shops and houses lining the wall inviting you to peek inside and explore them. The sound of seagulls and lapping water echoed through the room as they strolled down the wooden walkway towards the ship.

"Would you like to go aboard?" Rami asked, gesturing towards the narrow bridge leading to the ship. Savanah nodded in agreement. There were a few people milling about, but otherwise, the gallery was empty. A museum attendant greeted them and helped them aboard. Savanah looked up, surveyed the large sail and maze of ropes, and noticed Rami in her peripheral talking to the ship's attendant. The man smiled and glanced over to Savanah, making her wonder what they were discussing. Rami grinned at him and shook his hand, then returned to Savanah's side.

Savanah met his mischievous gaze and asked. "What are you up to?"

"Do you trust me?" Rami asked, his eyes dancing playfully with his question.

"You know I do," she replied with a smile curving her lips.

"Give me your hand," he said, taking her hand in his and bringing her closer. "Now close your eyes." Savanah hesitated, unsure of what he was going to do. "Go on." Rami encouraged, his eyes transfixed on hers. Savanah slowly closed her eyes as he turned her around and put his hands on her waist. Leading her a few steps forward, she could feel her footing angle on a slant, which she assumed was the bow of the ship. He leaned into her ear and whispered, "Step up." She stepped up hesitantly, her footing secure, and reached out in front of her to find the railing. "Hand on the railing," he encouraged, his breath hot in her ear. "Keep your eyes closed, don't peek."

"I won't," she answered, trepidation in her tone.

"Now lean forward, letting your weight rest on the railing. Trust me, you're safe. I got you," he said, his hands at her waist. "Do you trust me?" he asked again.

"I trust you," she whispered as he loosened her hold on the railing and brought her arms out wide, his grip on her secure and strong.

"Now open your eyes," he whispered in her ear, the warm tingle of his breath on her skin making her shiver in response.

She opened her eyes, immediately smiled, understanding what he was reenacting. The iconic scene on the bow of the ship in the movie *Titanic*. Playing the part of Rose, she exclaimed. "I'm flying, Rami, I'm flying!"

He planted a kiss on her cheek, his lean body at her back. He brought his hands down her extended arms, lacing his fingers with hers. They stayed like that for a minute, as if no one was there and it was just the two of them. Savanah brought her arms in, wrapping his powerful arms around her and turned her head to look up, her heart beating double time as it met his beautiful gaze. "Now this is romantic." She breathed out.

Rami's eyes twinkled as he lowered his mouth to hers for a long, languid, passionate kiss. Warmth spread through her body and settled in her core as her heart beat wildly in her chest. Everything about Rami awakened her senses and caused delicious tingles to spread throughout her body. The sound of someone clearing their throat broke them from their intimate embrace, reminding them they weren't alone. Rami grinned against her lips as he pulled away and helped her down from the bow of the ship. Savanah's face flushed, Rami took her hand in his and gave the smiling attendant a look of thanks as they disembarked the ship.

Savanah slipped her arm around his waist, and he draped his arm over her shoulder as they strolled out of the Nonsuch gallery, both lost in each other. They made their way through the rest of the museum talking, laughing, taking in the displays and stealing moments for PDA. When they had gone through the entire museum, they went downstairs to the planetarium to catch the last show of the evening and, as the galaxy of stars surrounded them, Savanah leaned in and whispered. "Can you sing me my song?"

Rami smirked and leaned into her, his warm breath creating goosebumps on her skin as he serenaded her softly in her ear.

RAMI AND SAVANAH both sat back in their chairs across from each other at an Italian restaurant overlooking the Red River. The night had fully descended, and the warm candlelight of the large dining room, along with rich dark wood walls, made the ambiance of the restaurant classically romantic and intimate.

Savanah placed a hand on her stomach, setting her fork down as she glanced down at her half-eaten plate of pasta and said, "I don't think I could eat another bite."

Rami smiled, completely captivated by the candlelight dancing in her stunning blue eyes. His heart was full, as he reached over and took her delicate hand in his, his thumb affectionately rubbing the skin between her thumb and index finger. His eyes lingered on their hands for a moment, relishing the feeling of this euphoric connection between them. Slowly, his gaze drifted up to meet hers as he spoke. "I really like you, Savanah."

"And I like you too, Rami. A lot," she confessed, her gaze affectionate and vulnerable. There was no denying the overwhelming connection and chemistry they shared. Every little look and every little touch, causing sparks to fly between them.

"I want you to know I'm all in on you." Rami continued, his face turning serious as he pinned her with his stare. "There's no one else, just you."

A slow smile curved Savanah's lips, and she trailed her hand over his forearm and back down to his hand, feathering her fingers with his as she asked. "What does that mean, then? Are we officially a thing?"

He flashed her his heart-stopping smile. "Do you want to be a thing?" he asked, stretching the word and making her giggle a little. "I mean, I would love for you to be my girlfriend, if that's the thing you're referring to."

Savanah bit her bottom lip with her teeth, her eyes dancing with the flicker of the candlelight as they transfixed on him and she replied. "I'd really like that."

Rami's heart filled with happiness as he leaned forward and brought her hand to his mouth and kissed it, his lips lingering a moment on the softness of her skin.

* * *

THE DRIVE BACK TO ST. Augustine was a quiet one, both tired and in a state of bliss and contentment. As Rami drove, Savanah couldn't help but look at the beautiful man next to her in the car. She had never met someone so sweet, thoughtful, and easy to be around. Everything about him drew her in, and she couldn't help but wonder where their relationship might go. Tonight, a switch had flipped, and she was ready to step into the role of Ramiro Perez's girlfriend. With this new label, she expected that intimacy would be on the table and although the thought of that made her nervous, she knew she was ready.

Savanah looked at him, surveying the angles of his handsome face, his long lashes, and his soft curly hair. She reached out and ran her fingers through his hair, needing to touch the soft curls. He leaned into her touch, an approving groan escaping his lips, the guttural sound making her core clench and pulse quicken. She couldn't remember ever being so wildly attracted to a man, and Rami was making her think of all the things she had yet to experience. All the things she wanted to experience with him.

Rami glanced at her, his eyes dark and delicious but his tone serious. "Savanah, I don't want you to think that I want to rush into intimacy with you, but the way you're looking at me right now is making me incredibly hot."

Savanah gave him a coquettish grin and removed her hands from his hair, setting them neatly on her lap as she confessed, "Sorry, you're just so darn handsome. I want to kiss you right now."

With her words, Rami quickly glanced in his rearview mirror and slowed, pulling over on the side of the highway. With a smile tugging at Savanah's lips, Rami put his car into park and unbuckled his seatbelt so he could turn to face her. Savanah did the same. Bringing his hands up around the back of her neck that was exposed from her hair being tied back in a ponytail, his fingers traced the line of her neck, before cupping her face and drawing close to kiss her. His lips were gentle as they moved over hers and she kissed him back with all the fervor he gave her. Feeling emboldened by the intensity surging between them, she traced the line of his lips with the tip of her tongue giving him an invitation to open and tangle with hers. Their kiss deepened as the passion quelled, and their tongues slid together. She moaned against his lips, adding fuel to the fire stoking between them. They kissed hungrily, consuming each other, losing track of time and place before they parted breathless, their faces flushed, and lips swollen.

Rami leaned back against his seat, his chest heaving, trying to catch his breath. Turning to face her, he smiled woozily. Her face was so hot she thought she might spontaneously combust, and her eyes were hazy with lust from their make-out session.

"I have never been kissed like that," she confessed, chest heaving, completely breathless.

He reached over and pressed his palm to her heated cheek affectionately. "There's plenty more where that came from. You are my girlfriend now, after all."

She smiled and covered his hand, cupping her cheek. "I like the sound of that."

CHAPTER 4

It had been three weeks since his last date with Savanah. Rami knew it was too long, and he felt bad that their schedules couldn't align. Although they talked every day either on the phone or via text, with his band doing gigs every weekend, their jobs and some drama between Garrett and Bea that thank goodness was resolved, they were long overdue for an official date. With their last one being so epic, he knew he needed to make this one stand out for her, and he needed to go to his source to find out where to start.

Rami walked into Primrose High School as many of the students turned their heads when he entered. A group of girls huddled and giggled when they saw him and most of the guys just gave him a once over trying to look cool. He checked in with the office, saw the sign for the chemistry lab near the front entrance exactly as Garrett had described. Approaching the door, Rami peeked inside. Garrett was seated at his desk, his brows furrowed with a stack of papers beside him and a red pen in hand.

"Hey, Garrett! Is this a good time?" Rami asked, entering his classroom.

Garrett looked up and smiled. "Yes, please. I've been grading these quizzes for the past hour." He replied, putting down the pen and getting up to greet Rami. He gestured to Rami to take a seat at one of the student tables and pulled a chair over to take a seat across from him. "Are you here for some advice on Savanah?" he asked with a big smile.

"Yeah, I want to take her on another romantic date, but I've started a theme here and feel a little stumped."

"You're recreating her favorite romantic movies, yes I remember." Garrett said thoughtfully as he nodded his head. "Pretty genius, actually." He commented, folding his arms over his chest as he took a moment to think. "You know, there is this movie that is literally her favorite movie of all time. I swear she's watched it hundreds of times and it's not as well known as your last two reenactments."

"Please tell me. I want this one to be extra special for her." Rami confessed, running his hand through his curly locks.

Garrett offered him a mischievous smile and asked, "Have you ever been to IKEA?"

* * *

SAVANAH WAS SO excited she could hardly contain herself. Dee had finally kicked her out of the shop, deeming her pacing and fidgeting both endearing and annoying. It had been far too long since she had spent time with

Rami and, although they communicated daily; she missed him terribly. With their last date being so memorable, she had no preconceived notions that all dates would be like that, but now with them making their relationship official, all she wanted was to spend time with him no matter what they did and what he had planned for them.

Their unbelievable kiss in his car last time played back in her mind like a film reel. Everything about it was hot and steamy, foreshadowing how good intimacy could be between them. It had awoken something in her she had never felt before, a desire to take things further. She was the first to admit she had zero experience in the bedroom. She had never been attracted enough to someone to take it there. However, with Rami, their history combined with and their intense chemistry, she had a feeling that intimacy had the potential to be like a scene out of one of her romance novels.

A knock sounded at her door, and she excitedly rushed down the short staircase towards her front entrance. She opened the door and was greeted by Rami's impossibly sexy smile. His arm braced against the doorjamb dressed in tight ripped black jeans, a brown V-neck T-shirt and a black leather jacket. Everything about his style screamed hot sexy rockstar.

"Well, hello there, pretty lady," he said in a playful suave tone, trying to sound like Elvis.

She returned his sexy smile, grabbed his jacket lapels, and brought him in for a long, hard, scorching kiss before releasing him. Lips still puckered; he slowly opened his eyes as a smile crept up his lips.

"I think you're happy to see me," he said, bringing her in for a hug.

Savanah wrapped her arms around him, inhaling his intoxicating scent as she whispered against his neck. "I missed you."

"I missed you too," he said, kissing her on the temple with affection. "Are you ready for date three in our epic romance series?"

"Yes, come in. I just need to get my boots on."

He followed her inside and up the stairs to the kitchen and living room area. "This is nice!" he commented, his eyes taking in her modest but modern space.

"Thanks, I'm proud of it. It was one of the first things I bought from the money I saved up from modeling. I wanted to own something rather than rent," she said as she reached for a pair or knee length suede brown boots and proceeded to pull them on.

Savanah could feel his eyes on her as he watched her slowly slide the zipper up her long, lean legs. She stood up straight and smoothed down the mauve pink thigh high sweater dress she was wearing.

"How can you always look so gorgeous?" he asked, taking in her short dress, boots and pink hair pulled to the side in waves. "I feel like the luckiest man in the world when I'm with you."

She offered him a modest smile and gave him a look of thanks as she reached for a brown suede crop jacket, which she had draped over one of her kitchen stools. He took it from her, surprising her, and gestured for her to turn around. Helping her into the jacket, Rami slipped it onto her shoulders and leaned down, planting a kiss on the exposed side of her neck. His tender kiss made electricity zing through her body, and she leaned back into him, closing her eyes, relishing the warmth of his affection. Rami leaned in further, his breath at her ear, "Let's go, mi novia."

* * *

THEY PULLED into the IKEA parking lot and Savanah's eyes grew wide. Seeing the big blue sign, she knew instantly why he had chosen this place. "Are we playing house?" she asked as she unbuckled her seatbelt.

He smiled, knowing she had put two and two together. "Perhaps we'll buy a fruge? I think we could use one."

Savanah giggled with excitement as she leaned in to give him a chaste kiss.

He helped her out of his car, and they walked hand in hand into the vast store. As they went up the escalators, he lifted her hand to kiss it and they strolled through the living room area first past the displays of couches. A living room scene was set up in a corner and he let go of her hand to round a couch and flop down, putting his feet up on the coffee table. "Home sweet home," he said with a sigh. Savanah knew *500 Days of Summer* word for word. She grinned and sat down next to him. "Our place really is lovely, isn't it?" she said breathlessly as she crossed her legs and reached for the fake television remote on the coffee table. "Oh, Idol's on." She continued, pretending to turn on the television. Rami laughed and snuggled up next to her. They sat there for a moment, pretending this was their living room, until she turned to him and put her lip out into a pout. "The TV's not working."

Rami mirrored her sad look, stretched his arm around her and said, "Oh, well, I'm famished. Let's eat!"

He got up from the couch and put his hand out to her, helping her up. He slid his arm around her waist as they passed the living room displays and entered the kitchens. Seeing one that looked nice, he took a seat at a kitchen table, picked up the fork and knife from the display and said, "Hmm… smells delicious."

Savanah pulled open the oven and, in a saccharine, sweet tone recited the line, "Oh, honey, that's because it *is* delicious!" She pretended to pull something out of the oven and put it on his plate. "I made it myself!"

Rami looked down with mock admiration and looked back up to her as he swung his cloth napkin in circles in the air. With a chuckle, he glanced up at her and, in a whisper, asked, "What's the next line?"

She leaned into his ear and answered, "Bald Eagle."

"That's right. Bald Eagle!" he repeated enthusiastically.

"Your favorite!" she giggled as she strode over to the sink, pretending to turn it on just like in the movie. "This sink isn't working." She said, feigning frustration with her hands on her hips.

Rami stood from his seat and said, "That's why we bought a home with two kitchens." He grabbed her hand and led her across the aisle into another kitchen display and brought her into his arms.

Savanah's pulse quickened at the feel of his hard body pressed to hers. She looked up through her thick lashes and whispered, "You are so smart." then wiggled out of his hold, skipping down the aisle, exclaiming playfully. "I'll race you to the bedroom."

Rami laughed and followed her until they were in the bedroom section. Savanah weaved in and out of the bedroom displays until she found one she liked and flopped onto the bed on her back, her head buried in the soft pillows. Rami crawled onto the bed, hovering over her, and she thought her heart may leap out of her chest. His brown eyes were dark and hooded, and she could see the desire for her in their depths. He purred out the last line from her favorite scene in her favorite movie. "Darlin', I don't know how to tell you this, but there's a Chinese family in our bathroom."

Savanah laughed as an older couple passed them, offering them a knowing smile as they both shook their heads. Rami flopped to the side onto the pillow to face her, and she cuddled up to him, their faces just a few inches apart. "This is fun, you are fun," she whispered, leaning in to seal her lips to his. He pulled her in by her waist till she was flush with his body, and he deepened their kiss, his tongue teasing hers.

A loud clearing of a throat sounded, and Rami released her lips, raising his head to find an IKEA employee with her hands on her hips and an amused smirk on her face. "*500 days of Summer?*" she asked. Rami nodded and Savanah buried her head in his chest to muffle the giggle threatening to escape.

They both rolled out of the bed, tried to smooth out the display, and apologized to the employee as they continued their stroll through the store, arms around each other as they went. While in the store they had dinner feeding each other Swedish meatballs and Savanah picked out a bookshelf, which Rami insisted on coming over right away to help her build. He declared building IKEA furniture together would help strengthen their budding relationship. Savanah couldn't agree more, as she didn't want their date to end.

When they got back to Savanah's, Rami pulled out the box which barely fit into the RX-7's trunk and followed her to the front door. She unlocked it, and he followed her up the stairs to the main living area.

"Where do you want this?" he asked, the box balancing on his shoulder.

"We can assemble it here and then we'll carry it into the bedroom." She answered, moving aside her coffee table to give them room for assembly.

He nodded, removed his jacket, and set to work as she poured them each a glass of wine. She handed him a glass, and he held his out to clink hers. She obliged. "To us," he said simply, then added. "And may the IKEA gods not test our relationship too much."

Savanah giggled and joined him in the living room, making herself comfortable on the couch as she watched him open the box, pulled out the instructions and handed them to her. She admired him as she walked him through the assembly, step by step, enjoying the flex of his muscles as he worked. At one point, he stood up and stretched out his back, his t-shirt rising to reveal his taut stomach and the hint of a sexy v-cut at his hips. She found herself biting her bottom lip as her eyes roamed over his smooth, tanned skin.

He caught her checking him out and he flashed her his

most devilish smile then shook his head as he took a sip of his wine and said, "Savanah Smithfield, if you keep looking at me that way, I may not want to leave."

"Who says you have to?" She answered boldly, looking up at him through her thick lashes.

He met her gaze, a flash of desire within their chocolate depths, and nervously raised the glass of wine to his lips, taking another sip before he continued his assembly of the bookshelf.

Taking in his reaction to her flirtation, at first Savanah chided herself for her brazen comment, but when she continued to watch him, she noticed he appeared nervous. The stark realization that he was affected by her as much as she was affected by him hit her hard. She had never felt like she had that kind of power over a man and always came across as the anxious, nervous one. She wasn't used to eliciting that powerful reaction in someone else.

He finished putting together her bookshelf and flopped down on the couch next to her, a look of accomplishment on his face. She took a sip of her wine; the liquid giving her courage to ask him the question that replayed in her mind over the past half hour.

"Do you want to be with me?" she asked, imploring him to answer honestly.

He twisted his head to hers and met her questioning gaze, surprise on his face. A smile tugged at his lips as he answered, "Of course."

She smiled and relaxed against the couch cushions, feeling a sense of relief. He turned his body to face her and ran his hand over her knee, resting on her thigh. "I just don't want you to think that's all I want. You literally have my head spinning when I am around you. I want you that much, Savanah."

Savanah smiled and reached over, running her fingers through his soft curls. "I don't think I've ever felt this way about anyone." She confessed, meeting his tender gaze. "All I want is to be wrapped up in your arms."

"I can do that," he answered, his gaze honest and pure. "I don't want you to feel pressured to do more, though. I'm happy to just hold you tonight."

"I'd like that," she said, intertwining her fingers with his and glancing at the kitchen clock. "It's after 1 a.m. and I would feel terrible sending you home at this hour."

"Then I'll stay," he said, brushing a chaste kiss to her lips. "Let's get this bookshelf to your room and get ready for bed."

Together, they carried the bookshelf down the hall to her bedroom and set it in the corner. Rami glanced around her room and nodded his approval at the large space. The queen size bed was modern with a grey bed frame and tall upholstered headboard. It was dressed beautifully in plush soft linens in a light shade of pink and a variety of decorative pillows in various textures and shades of pink and cream. Her bed was cozy and inviting. A tall dresser stood in the corner opposite where they set the bookshelf, and she had a large walk-in closet next to the door of the ensuite. Savanah opened a drawer and pulled out a pair of silky pajamas. She looked at Rami and furrowed her brow. "I don't have anything to give you to sleep in."

"I always sleep in my boxers if you're okay with that."

Savanah gave him a timid nod, her pulse going up a few notches thinking about him half naked in her bed. She slipped into the ensuite and changed into her silky button-down shirt and short pajama set, tossing her clothes into the hamper. She opened the door and found Rami already shirtless, his lean long tanned torso making her breath catch. *God, he's beautiful.* Her mouth suddenly dry, she swallowed nervously and met his eyes as she spoke. "I have an extra toothbrush if you want to brush your teeth."

Rami smiled softly and followed her into the ensuite standing beside her at her single sink. She unwrapped a new toothbrush and handed it to him, along with the toothpaste. He gave her a grateful look, loaded his toothbrush with toothpaste, and handed it back to her so she could do the same. They brushed their teeth together, both watching each other's reflection in the mirror across from the sink. The entire moment feeling intimate and domestic. Rami spit and rinsed off his brush, and she followed, placing her brush in the holder, and holding out her hand to take his brush, putting it in the spot next to hers. She grabbed a hairbrush and gathered her hair up into a messy bun at the top of her head, securing it with a scrunchie. She removed her makeup with a cloth and noticed him leaning against the door frame, watching her. Something about the way he looked at her was sweet and sensual. Like he was truly seeing the woman she was within. When she was done, she glanced in the mirror at him and he came around her back, his hands on her waist, and leaned in, placing a gentle kiss on her neck.

"Let's go to bed," he whispered, taking her hand, and

leading her to the bed. They removed all the pillows, and he pulled back the covers as she climbed onto the bed, crawling to her side and slipping under the covers. She watched as he undid his belt, pulling it out and setting it on the nightstand. Popping the button on his jeans, he slipped them down his legs, then off. Savanah took in his strong thighs and cinched cut waist, willing her eyes not to drift down lower to the noticeable bulge.

Rami slipped in next to her, the warmth of his body a direct contrast to the cold covers. He pulled her close to him, her feet finding his, and he let out a chuckle. "Your feet are so cold."

"They always are," she giggled, running her foot over his warm calf.

A grin on his lips, he reached up and smoothed a strand of hair that had escaped her bun, then ran his hands down the contours of her cheekbones and across the bridge of her nose and under her eyes.

"I love your freckles." He whispered, his brown eyes warm and sleepy. She scrunched up her nose, and he chuckled, low and soft. "You're just so beautiful, Savanah. Inside and out."

Savanah felt his words with such sweetness and sincerity. She was terrible at receiving compliments, especially from men. But when Rami said it, warmth radiated through her. He saw her, the real her and liked everything about her. Savanah's heart was full and Rami's warm breath caressing her cheek she closed her eyes and fell into a peaceful sleep.

CHAPTER 5

Rami watched Savanah sleep; her silky pink hair having slipped out of the bun was now spread out across her pillow. She looked so tranquil and angelic; her face soft, glowing, perfection. He had never seen anyone so incredibly beautiful. Last night, feeling the blissful warmth of her body next to his, something shifted within him, and he knew he was falling in love with her. The only problem was, he had no idea if she was feeling the same. Yes, he knew she liked him; she liked him a lot, that was very apparent, but love, he was clueless when it came to her. *Am I willing to put my feelings out there to find out? Will I be okay if she's not in the same place as me?*

Savanah's eyes fluttered, and they opened sleepily. He loved her eyes, the color of ocean blue so large and expressive, framed with lush thick lashes. She smiled; her lips half covered by her pillow. "Were you watching me?" she asked, tilting her head to fully face him.

"A little," he replied, reaching up and slipping a strand

of her pink hair over her ear. "You're just so cute when you sleep."

She scrunched up her nose and asked, "What do you mean?"

"You flutter your eyes a lot, and you smile in your sleep."

"That's not too bad," she giggled. "I thought you were going to say I snore or make weird or obscene noises."

A deep chuckle rumbled from Rami's chest as he asked teasingly, "Savanah, have you been having naughty dreams about me?"

Rami expected her shy smile and her usual blush to tint her cheeks, but Savanah met his gaze and cocked an eyebrow at him, replying, "I can neither confirm nor deny."

Rami's pulse quickened as he slid his hand over her waist, her pajama shirt having ridden up slightly, leaving a line of bare skin. His fingers traced back and forth along that ribbon of flesh, and she squirmed, then shivered, making them both smile. *My God, her skin is soft.* His desire for her rose as his hand slid over her bare back. Her hand slid over his side too, exploring the contours and ridges of his arms and shoulders, then around to his back, tracing his spine. Something about lying with her, together, staring into each other's eyes, just touching each other with reverence and discovery made their connection feel incandescent. They lay like that for a long time, taking each other in, and Rami knew this was the moment he needed to tell her.

"Savanah, I'm falling in love with you," he whispered,

vulnerability edging his declaration. "And I understand if you're not there yet, but..."

Savanah reached up and cupped his face, bridging the gap between them as she kissed him, gentle and tender. Pulling back to gaze into his eyes, she replied, "I'm falling for you too."

THEY SPENT the morning snuggled up together in bed, talking, laughing, touching, and kissing. Simply relishing the timid beginnings of intimacy and the burgeoning feelings of love.

Losing track of time, the noon hour struck and both, now starving, rolled out of bed. Rami took a shower while Savanah fixed them some lunch. He emerged from her room, his upper body bare, and his beltless jeans sitting low on his narrow hips. Savanah couldn't help but bite her lip as she took him in with appreciation. "Are ham and cheese sandwiches, okay?" she asked, as she sliced up carrots putting them on the side of each plate.

"Perfect." he said, taking a seat at the island.

She slid a plate with a sandwich and a handful of carrot sticks on the side over to him and he picked up a half, taking a big bite and giving her a thumbs up.

"I'm not exactly a cook," she said, grabbing a carrot stick and snapping off a bite. "But I can make sandwiches."

"That's okay. I know how to cook."

"You do?" she asked, lifting half of her sandwich.

"Yes." he chuckled. "I wouldn't be a Perez if I didn't. I mean, my Abuela owns the Blue Corn, Marnie is a masterful baker, and we have these huge weekly family dinners where everyone pitches in and cooks together."

"That sounds amazing."

"Speaking of my family and our dinners, they gather every Sunday at my Abuela's. It's always a big feast and of course the food is amazing. Would you like to go with me tonight?" he asked, hope shimmering in his eyes.

Savanah blinked, completely flattered to be invited. It was a big step to meet his entire family and although she'd already had the opportunity to meet Abuela and Marnie, she had no idea at the time that they were related. This would be the first time meeting his family as his girl-friend. She looked into his questioning eyes. *How can I possibly say no?* "I would love that, Rami. Thank you." He beamed at her, leaned in and kissed her gently, making butterflies awaken in her belly.

They cleaned up the dishes together and went back to her bedroom, making the bed together. Savanah wanted every day to be like this, Rami here in her home with her. To her, just having him be in her space was incredibly intimate.

"Do you want to wash your clothes? I assume you don't have anything else to wear with you." she asked. "You probably weren't expecting to spend the night."

"Sure, but what could I wear in the meantime?" he laughed, as he glanced over to her walk-in closet. "Pretty sure anything of yours wouldn't fit me."

Savanah giggled at that and tapped a finger on her

chin for a moment, then went into the hallway, rummaging through a closet, reappearing with a flat sheet. "Would this do?"

"Are we having a toga party?" he asked with a raised brow.

"Well, you are at least!" she laughed, handing him the sheet, turning him and nudging him towards her ensuite. "Go in there, strip down, and give me a fashion show!"

"Challenge accepted!" he exclaimed, doing as she ordered.

Savanah climbed onto the bed, crossing her legs as she waited for him to emerge.

"Look number one!" he announced, coming out of the ensuite. He had the sheet fashioned to his body like a toga and he strutted in front of her as if on a runway. "This is the classic toga look, of course."

"Solid choice. What else have you got?"

Rami ducked back into the ensuite and within a few minutes he announced, "Look number two!"

He came out with the sheet fashioned like a long sleeveless dress. Savanah giggled as he strutted and showed her his long, muscular leg through a slit on the side.

"Very sexy!" she laughed. "Got anything else?"

"I think I have one more look for you to consider," he said, giving her a wink before he slipped into the ensuite. A few minutes later, he announced, "I think I outdid myself with look number three. Are you ready?"

The door opened and Rami emerged from the ensuite with the flat sheet fashioned like the uniform of a sumo wrestler. Savanah fell back giggling hysterically as he strutted the runway, owning the look. Rami stood before her in a warrior pose as Savanah choked on tears of laughter. With a narrowed gaze and grin tugging at his lips, he stalked over to her and climbed onto the bed, hovering over her. His half naked state and the weight of his body making her core pulsate and body flush instantly. She stopped laughing as he leaned down and kissed her passionately. She matched him, her lips moving with his, her desire for him rising at a rapid pace. Before he could deepen their embrace, he released their kiss and fell back on the bed, letting out a long-pained groan. Savanah lay next to him, trying to catch her breath. He intertwined his hands with hers and brought her hand up to his lips to kiss it. Savanah smiled and said, "Let me show you where the laundry is."

* * *

REALIZING Abuela lived only a few blocks from Savanah in the same new development, they opted to walk there.

"I'm so nervous." Savanah confessed as they walked down the sidewalk hand in hand. "Which is weird since I've already met your Abuela and of course I know Marnie, it's just…"

"It's a big step to meet your boyfriend's family," he finished her thought. "I get it. I've never brought a woman home to meet them before."

Savanah stopped in her tracks, looking up at him with trepidation. "You know that doesn't make me feel any better, right?"

Rami laughed and pulled her in, planting a kiss on her temple. "My family is loud and crazy, but they're also very kind and welcoming. They will love you," he reassured, looking into her eyes. "I care so much about you; Savanah and they're going to be thrilled that I've found someone so special to me."

Savanah reached up, caressing his cheek. "You are so wonderful, Rami."

"I try," he replied with a wink as he leaned down and planted a chaste kiss on her lips. "Now stop worrying, my family is awesome."

* * *

SAVANAH COULDN'T BELIEVE the hospitality of the Perez family. Coming from a family with just her parents and her much older brother, she sometimes felt like an only child, with Garrett having gone off to college when she was still in elementary school. Now, in this house with more siblings, cousins, aunts, and uncles than she could have ever imagined having, she couldn't help but feel the closeness and warmth of his big, loving family.

Marnie, having been surprised and delighted to see her there, took a seat next to her as Rami was persuaded to pick up a guitar and play for everyone. He sat in the middle of the large living room, surrounded by family, and played a Spanish song, his fingers sweeping over the strings expertly. Savanah was transfixed watching him play.

"I sometimes can't believe how good he is." Marnie

mused. "He has always been a natural musician. Did you know he's never taken lessons? He is 100% self-taught."

Savanah glanced at Marnie, her eyes wide with surprise and then back to her boyfriend, strumming the guitar with precision as he sang. He looked up, meeting her gaze, flashing her his endearing smile, and making her heart flip flop. Savanah knew at that moment that she wasn't just falling, but was unquestionably in love with Rami Perez.

* * *

"HAVE A GREAT DAY," Rami said as an elderly couple left the bakery, a box of goodie in hand. He grabbed a dish-cloth and rounded the counter to wipe tables.

Savanah had been consuming his thoughts all day, and all he could think about was the night he spent with her in his arms. *Seriously, you're going to see her this weekend! Stop acting like a lovesick fool.* He couldn't help it. Every time his mind drifted off, he could see her ocean blue eyes and feel the softness of her lips on his. His hands ached to touch her skin and smooth down her silky hair. Everything about her drew him in and the realization that his feelings were entering the next stage was both scary and exhilarating.

"Rami." Marnie called as she peeked out of the back kitchen and spotted him. He didn't respond, and she shook her head as she exclaimed, "Earth to Rami!"

"Oh, sorry, what?" he asked, turning around to face her.

Marnie came out of the kitchen with her arms folded

over her chest and a knowing smirk on her lips. "Were you thinking about Savanah?"

Rami walked around the front counter, past his sister, and ran his hands through his hair as he asked. "Am I that obvious?"

Marnie laughed as Rami leaned on the counter. "Just a little." She replied as she slid in next to him and gave him a hip bump.

Rami met Marnie's gaze as he confessed, "I think I'm in love with her."

Marnie offered him a soft smile, her eyes sincere and supportive. "Do you think she's in love with you?"

Rami let his eyes drift to the picture window over-looking the Main Street of Primrose as he took in Marnie's question, then looked back at his sister, replying, "I think she is."

Marnie stood up straight and clapped him on the back. "Then you, my dear brother, need to tell her."

"HAVE A GREAT DAY!" Savanah exclaimed as a customer left her shop, a bag in hand. She turned to the dressing room and shouted, "Dee, are you going to show me what you picked?"

The dressing room door flung open and Dee, wearing a long colorful floral kimono style robe, black tank top and black jeans with black suede booties, emerged, did a little turn and posed for Savanah.

"Oh, my gosh, I love the robe! Are you going to wear it on Saturday night?" she asked, grabbing a rancher style hat and putting it on Dee's head. She posed in the mirror and Savanah commented, "The hat is perfect."

Dee nodded in agreement and turned around to face Savanah. "I'm kind of excited about this weekend. I haven't seen Rami's band yet and I'm not going to lie, I'm curious. I tried looking online for videos or social media posts, but there was next to nothing out there."

"You're going to love them, Dee!" she said, perusing the necklace display and picking one out for Dee's outfit. "Rami is so talented."

"And gorgeous." Dee added with a grin.

"And sexy." Savanah murmured on a sigh. "Oh, Dee, I think I'm in love with him."

Dee turned and surveyed her, a slow smile curving her lips. "Are you serious?"

Savanah nodded, giving her best friend a look of certainty. "I've never felt this way about anyone. My stomach gets all fluttery when I'm around him and he makes me feel so wonderful whenever we're together. Like he sees all of me, not just the outside, but who I am in here." She placed her hand over her heart. "All I want is to be with him all the time. Dee, it's so intense, it's hard to describe."

"Well, that sounds like love to me," Dee replied, walking over and wrapping her in a hug before holding her out at arm's length and asking. "And do you know how he feels?"

"I think he loves me, too. When I look in his eyes, I see it, but we haven't said the words yet. We confessed that we're falling, but we haven't said *I love you*, yet. I'm so scared to say it first, Dee. What if he's not there yet?" she said, covering her face with her hands.

"Stop, Savanah. You always do that. You always second guess yourself." She said, resting her hand on Savanah's shoulder. "Trust your instincts and trust your heart."

Dee was right. If Savanah was in love with Rami, she needed to trust that Rami would reciprocate, even if it meant putting her heart on the line.

CHAPTER 6

It was a cool October night, the kiss of winter on the horizon when Savanah and Dee walked into the Pickled Pig, a popular honky tonk bar that had become a favorite of the locals and neighboring towns around St. Augustine. With its cheesy décor, awesome dance floor and incredible drink specials, it was the place to be on the weekend. Now offering live bands twice a month, tonight, Prairie Sound was the headliner, and the bar was packed.

Surveying the space, Savanah spotted two seats at the corner of the bar not yet occupied. "Let's grab those seats before the show starts." She shouted to Dee over the loud music.

They weaved their way through the crowd, most of which were standing and milling closer to the stage at the other end of the room. Savanah, never much for large crowds, preferred to watch from a distance, so she was happy to find a safe place for them to sit and listen.

"Can I get you ladies a drink?" a devilishly handsome

middle-aged Bartender asked, giving them both a look over, not hiding his obvious approval of the beautiful young woman in front of him.

"Two Cosmos!" Dee shouted, unapologetically checking out the silver fox in return. Dee had always had a thing for older men, and it wasn't uncommon for her to give no mind to an age gap.

The bartender flirtatiously gave her a wink and asked, "What brings you beautiful ladies out tonight? Are you here to see the band?"

They both nodded and Dee responded, "My friend, Savanah here is the lead singer's girlfriend!"

He did a once over on Savanah with her high pink ponytail, black leather jacket, cropped AC/DC t-shirt, pink tulle skirt and black fringed boots. Savanah, without question, looked the part of a rocker's girlfriend. "Ah, so you're Rami's girl? He mentioned you would be here tonight. Nice to meet you. I'm Sylvio Conti and I own this establishment. Anything you ladies want is on me!" he said with a flash of his swoony smile as he set their drinks in front of them. They both smiled graciously and thanked him as he moved to the next customer.

Dee picked up her drink, turned and brought it to her lips, taking a sip, then commented with a nod of approval, "Delicious drinks, hot bartender, awesome band. This is going to be a good night."

Savanah giggled, taking a sip of her cocktail as well and clinked her glass with Dee in agreement. Having drawn the attention of the opposite sex, a couple of men were starting to circle when the crowd parted, and Rami appeared dressed in a blue V-neck t-shirt, tight black ripped jeans, a flannel shirt tied around his narrow waist, combat boots and his signature leather cuffs. He was flagged by his three bandmates, Layne, Steve and Rex. Rami flashed her his gorgeous panty dropping smile as he zoned in on her. He swooped her up into his arms and planted a hot sexy kiss on her lips, at first surprising her before she melted in his arms.

Pulling his lips away before they got too carried away by their PDA, he rested his forehead against hers and sucked in a breath, as he whispered low and deep, "I missed you, mi novia."

"I missed you too," she replied with a breath, completely intoxicated by the heady swirl of lust and love he evoked in her.

Setting her back down on her feet, her face piqued with rosiness, he turned her, arms still wrapped around her as he made introductions.

"Guys, this is my girlfriend Savanah." he said, planting a kiss on her temple. "And her best friend Dee Jones." His bandmates nodded their smiles wide. "Ladies, these are my bandmates, Layne Stark, who plays base..." he said, gesturing to a handsome blonde with soft, kind brown eyes. "Steve Furgallo, our keyboardist..." he continued, introducing a handsome, very tall, slender man with long black hair, midnight eyes, and a sweet smile. "And this is the infamous Rex Johnson, who is our drummer," he concluded by nodding to a tattooed, beefy man with a blue mohawk and eyes to match.

"Well, hello indeed." Rex greeted raucously, sidling up close to Dee.

In pure, emboldened Dee fashion, she raised her

eyebrow at him, her eyes twinkling with mirth as she commented, "Nice mohawk, drummer boy."

"Thanks, the ladies seem to like it," Rex said, giving her a gentle nudge and waggling his eyebrows at her.

"Rex likes to think he's a ladies' man." Layne teased. "The operative word here is *thinks*."

The entire group laughed, and Rex just ignored his comment with a shrug and another flirtatious waggle of his brows at Dee.

The stage lights came up, grabbing the attention of the band. "Looks like it's time to start." Steve said to Rami and the rest of the band. "Nice to meet you ladies," he said, offering them a kind smile before he, Layne and Rex disappeared into the crowd, headed towards the stage.

"It gets pretty crazy up front, so here is a great place to stay," Rami whispered to Savanah, before giving her another chaste kiss and following his bandmates towards the stage.

They both watched them go and Dee's midnight eyes met Savanah's as she commented, "That man is completely gone on you, girl."

Savanah smiled. So many of her questions answered with his greeting to her tonight. She was certain that Rami was as much in love with her as she was in love with him. Nervousness bloomed in her belly as she tamped down her self-doubt and promised herself, *I'm going to tell him.*

"How are you all doing tonight?" Rami shouted into the mic. The bar roared back in response. "We're Prairie Sound and I hope you're all ready to rock." The energy in the bar lifting the roof.

The spotlight shone on Rami as he went into the familiar classic U2 guitar solo of "Where the Streets Have No Name." and his bandmates took their places gradually adding Rex on the drums, Layne on bass and Steve on keyboards. The tempo building, the crowd pressing the stage with mounting energy, ready to erupt. Rami smiled and stepped to the mic belting out the first line, and the bar went wild.

Sylvio leaned into Savanah and Dee from across the bar and exclaimed, "Fuck, they're good!"

Dee smiled widely and nodded in agreement, her eyes dancing. Savanah was transfixed on Rami, commanding the stage, his deep masculine voice with its edgy rasp caressing the song. Even being across the room, the energy of the crowd made her pulse quicken and heart beat out of her chest. *My boyfriend is phenomenal!*

The band played a combination of covers by Rock legends like Bon Jovi, Van Halen and Whitesnake, Alt rock covers from the Cure, Nirvana, and Fall Out Boy and some originals threaded within, keeping the crowd entertained throughout. As the concert wound down, Rami came to the center of the small stage, his T-shirt stained with sweat, and set two stools down, facing the crowd. He took a seat on one of the stools and adjusted the mic to his level, then said, "I got one more special song to sing tonight, for someone that means everything to me. I sing it at every concert, and the reason I sing it is because it's her favorite. Savanah, mi novia, come sit next to me while I sing it for you and all these amazing people!"

Savanah's eyes widened in surprise, and her face

flushed crimson red as Dee nudged her, "He wants you up there on stage."

"Make room for my girl." Rami gestured for the packed crowd to make a path for her to come through.

A security guard appeared at her side and said, "This way." as he parted the crowd and Savanah followed him hesitantly towards the stage. The guard offered her a hand to help her onto the raised platform and Rami stepped up to take her hand, his acoustic guitar slung to the side.

His smile was wide as he took in the surprised look on her face and leaned in to whisper in her ear. "Ask me to sing your song."

Meeting his gorgeous chocolate eyes, reflecting the spotlights, she cocked an eyebrow at him as she asked sweetly, "Rami, can you please sing me my song?"

Bringing her hand to his lips, he kissed it, then led her to the stool next to his. She took a seat, the stage lights blinding, but she could still make out the sea of faces watching them. With a fluttery feeling in her belly, she gazed at Rami, who flashed her a reassuring wink. He leaned into the mic as he turned, meeting her with eyes so soft and sweet as he declared. "This one's for you, Savanah, because I love you."

You could hear the ladies in the crowd either swoon or groan at his words, but they were just white noise after his confession to her here on this stage. She reached out and touched his face tenderly, her gaze searching the depths of his brown eyes so full of love and adoration for her. He loved her and she loved him. "I love you too, Rami." she confirmed, a swell of overwhelming sentiment edging her voice. The look in his eyes was a combination of pure elation and glistening emotion. The familiar keyboards sounded behind her, and Rami strummed his guitar as he leaned into the mic, singing the first line. He glanced her way, a beautiful smile curving his lips as he serenaded her in front of the enrapt crowd.

* * *

AFTER THE CONCERT, Savanah returned to her seat next to Dee, and she gushed about the concert, Sylvio joining in on their conversation.

"I don't know how Prairie Sound hasn't been picked up by a label yet," Sylvio shared, over the music. "I mean, they're incredibly talented, each one of them stellar performers and every time they play here, this place is packed, and the crowd goes crazy."

"Do they do anything on social media, uploading videos to YouTube, TikTok or anything like that?" Dee asked curiously.

Sylvio shook his head. "There may be some pictures or videos floating around of their performances, but nothing uploaded to any platforms like YouTube. The band needs exposure. I just don't think any of them know where to begin with that."

"Well, I can help a little. It's not my area of expertise but I have helped Savanah here with her boutiques website and social media and did some marketing for social media courses in university."

"Why don't you start with the concert footage you took tonight? Seriously, these kids need their big break.

They're ready to take off!" Sylvio added as he moved on, helping another bartender with a large order.

Savanah turned to Dee and asked curiously, "Did you record part of the concert?"

Dee nodded and pulled out her phone, showing her a small clip of what she took. "I even have Rami singing to you on stage." She added with a wink. "That may have been the sweetest profession of love I've ever seen. And now we have it on video."

Savanah smiled wistfully, thinking about it. *It was perfect.* "Can you send me the video?"

Dee nodded and smiled knowingly at her best friend as she glanced back down at her phone.

Warm hands rounded her waist, and familiar lips met the sensitive skin beside her ear. His intoxicating cologne, along with manly musky sweat met her, and she breathed deeply, gripping his hands on her, and leaning back against his hard, toned body. "I love you," he whispered in her ear, making her close her eyes as waves of love and desire washed over her.

She sighed and turned in his arms to meet his soft and tender gaze. "I love you, too." She said, taking his face in her hands and planting a long, languid kiss on his lips.

A hoot and a whistle sounded next to them, and they parted, Rami holding her securely to his chest. Rex, Layne, Steve, and Dee were watching them with looks of pure amusement on their faces.

"If you two are done sucking face, can we split and get something to eat?" Rex asked gruffly.

"There's a late-night diner in St. Augustine." Layne shared, glancing between their group.

"Will you ladies be joining us?" Steve asked, giving Savanah a chaste look, then drifting to Dee and pinning her with his obsidian stare.

Rex put his arm around Dee possessively squinting at Steve telling him to back off and Dee removed his arm slowly. Just then, a group of three girls passed Rex and a busty blonde slid her fingers over his arm seductively, flashing him a sultry smile. "Well, hello ladies!" he said, following them and putting his arm around the blonde.

"And we lost Rex," Layne said with a grin and a shrug. "How about the rest of you?"

"I'm game," Dee replied, holding her hand up.

"Me too." answered Steve.

The three friends looked at Rami, whose arm was over Savanah's shoulder and her arm securely around his waist. "We'll come for a short while, but not long. We want to spend some time alone."

Savanah felt her cheeks warm at his response and her body instantly reacted to the thought of them being alone and all that time alone implied. With their love for each other declared, Savanah was ready to take their relationship further and didn't want to hold back any longer.

* * *

As PROMISED, Rami and Savanah spent the next hour with their friends at the Diner. Rami's finger found the exposed skin of her outer thigh just above her skirt as he trailed his fingers lightly over her skin, causing her to feel lightheaded and woozy as desire pooled low in her belly. They had both been half listening to the conversation

Layne and Steve were having with Dee about setting up social media accounts for the band and posting their videos. Rather, all their attention was on the building sexual tension between them. She leaned into his ear, whispering for only him to hear. "Will you come home with me tonight?"

His eyes searched hers and darkened as he asked, "Are you sure?"

"More than sure. I want to be with you," she admitted, the words escaping on a breath as she gazed into his searching eyes.

Rami sprang from the table, and everyone turned, watching him as he pulled Savanah up with him. "We're going to split." Rami croaked, need edging his tone as he laced his fingers with Savanah's.

"Before you guys take off, let me talk to Savanah for a moment." Dee said, getting up from their table and pulling Savanah to a quiet nook near the bathrooms. When they were sure no one was in earshot, she pinned Savanah with her eyes and asked, "Is tonight the night?"

Savanah nodded, sliding her hands down her tulle skirt nervously and rocking back and forth in her fringed boots. Her brows drew together, and she asked, "Are you okay here with the Layne and Steve?"

"Yeah, of course, they're sweet guys." Dee replied, feigning her concern with a wave of her hand as she gripped Savanah's shoulders and gave her a supportive smile. "Have fun and text me tomorrow. Rami is one in a million and I'm so happy for you, Savanah." she said, pulling her in for a hug. "Love you, girl."

"Love you too," Savanah replied, hugging her best

friend before they strolled back to the table. Rami met her gaze as he took her hand and threaded his fingers with hers, a look of knowing on his face as they left the diner together.

* * *

ARRIVING AT SAVANAH'S TOWNHOME, they strolled to her door as she reached into her purse, fumbling for her keys. Savanah's hands trembled with nervousness and the embarrassment of how incredibly anxious she was, made her audibly sigh. Frustrated, she looked down at her hands and leaned against the stucco wall of the front stoup alcove. Rami's brows drew together as he searched her gaze, his eyes filled with gentle sincerity as he took her shaking hands in his, smoothing his thumbs over her knuckles.

"You know we don't have to do this, if you're not ready," he reassured, with deep affection. "I can wait as long as you need."

Her eyes drifted from their hands up to his sincere gaze, and she shook her head. "I want this, Rami. I want this with you. I love you." She said quickly, feeling the need to reassure him she wasn't second guessing her desire for him. "It's just that I've never done this before." She confessed tentatively, looking up at him, her pulse quickening, unsure of his response.

His lips curled into his endearing lopsided smile as she gazed down at her with tender affection. Reaching up, he caressed his palm over her cheek and answered, "What if I told you I haven't, either?"

Savanah's eyes widened as she responded incredulously, "Really?"

"Really." he replied, his eyes never leaving hers as his fingers traced the silhouette of her face and he tucked a stray strand of hair behind her ear. "I mean doing what I do, I've been propositioned more than my share, but I have never been interested in meaningless sex. I wanted to give that part of me to someone I care deeply about and love," he explained, his eyes soft and radiating the love he declared to her on stage. "Savanah, I have never cared for anyone more than I care for you. I love you so much. I want to experience everything with you."

Savanah searched his eyes, to be met with pure honesty. Never did the scenario of them both being virgins cross her mind. They were both 23 and although she knew by modern standards that was old for her to still be a virgin, to find a man that shared her same convictions and valued the meaning behind sharing this ultimate form of intimacy, was rare. Let alone a confident man that could command a crowd on stage and had women throw themselves at him all the time. That was the nature of what he did, so never did she have illusions that he had chosen to save himself like she had. A scorching fire of desire burned low in her belly. *I want him.* Taking in a calming breath, she reached into her purse and found her keys, then looked up into his lustful eyes. "It's cold, let's go inside."

Savanah unlocked the door and took his hand, leading him up the stairs to her kitchen and living room. They both took off their jackets, hung them on the backs of the kitchen stools, and she led him towards her bedroom. He unlaced his combat boots and Savanah removed her boots, slipping into her walk-in closet putting them on a shelf. Rami's hands were on her waist before she could turn around.

"Do you mind if I take a quick shower?" he asked, his breath hot on her cheek.

"Not at all. Go ahead." She replied, her voice coming out rough and raspy with her mounting need. "I'm just going to get changed."

The heat of hands left her body, and she immediately felt cold, the need to feel him close to her, his hands roaming over her skin, palpable. Last time he spent the night, she simply got a taste, but tonight she was going to have the entire meal. She took a deep calming breath to steady her nerves, as she reached for the beautiful lace and silk nightgown hanging in front of her. She had bought it two years ago, thinking it was so pretty, with its dusty rose color and delicate lace bust. It made her feel pretty and sexy when she tried it on and even though she didn't have anyone in her life at the time to wear it for; she hoped someday she would wear it for someone special. Savanah stripped off all her clothes and slipped on the silky nightgown, loving how it hugged her small curves and barely kissed her bare skin with its softness. She exited her closet, closing the doors when she heard the shower stop, and she nervously took a seat on the bed, not sure what to do with her hands while she waited for him to emerge. Quickly, she pulled her hair out of the ponytail, sliding her fingers through the long strands. The ensuite door opened, a cloud of steam escaping and Rami walked out with nothing but a towel around his narrow hips. Savanah thought her heart may stop at the sight of him. Her eyes roamed down his body, his strong shoulders, muscular arms, beautiful chest, and flat, toned stomach. The cut V at his hips drew her eyes down before they darted up to meet his sultry gaze. His eyes were dark and lustful, the eyes of a man ready to show his girlfriend how much he loved her.

RAMI APPROACHED her and reached his hand out to Savanah, pulling her up from the bed. He held her out in front of him, taking in the silky nightgown she had changed into. It was gorgeous, accentuating the swells of her breasts, the semi sheer lace teasing what was underneath. The soft material just skimmed her lean, long body, which he was aching to touch.

"You take my breath away," he rasped wantonly, his hands settling on her waist. She reached up, looping her hands around his neck, her fingers running through his wet curls, making him groan with approval. "That feels so good Savanah, I want you to tell me what feels good for you, okay?"

"Okay." she agreed as his hands on her waist slid up over her sides towards her breasts, his hands settled on their underside waiting for her okay to keep going. "Touch me, Rami." she whispered. With her words, his hands cupped her breasts, kneading the soft flesh, his thumbs teasing their peaks. A small moan escaped her throat as he leaned down and kissed the side of her neck and down over her collarbone. "That feels so good," she whimpered; her head thrown back.

My God, she tastes so good. His tongue teased the hollow of her neck and then back to her lips for a soft, sultry kiss. He turned, the edge of her bed hitting the backs of his legs, forcing him to sit. She looked down at him; her mesmerizing blue eyes were full of love and overflowing desire as his hands found the hem of her nightgown and roamed underneath, lightly caressing over the bare flesh of her impossibly long legs. His hands rounded over the curve of her behind and her breath hitched as goose-bumps formed on her skin.

"Does this feel good?" he asked, his hands kneading the soft, supple skin. She nodded and reached for the hem of her nightgown. He removed his hands and leaned back as she drew the nightgown slowly up her body, inch by glorious inch, exposing pale, flawless skin. With one swift move, she pulled the gown over her head, letting the delicate garment drift to the floor, leaving her completely revealed to him. He sat up, his eyes unabashedly taking in her long lean body with soft, subtle womanly curves that made his mouth dry as he drank in the perfection of her. His eyes drifted up to hers, hazy with lust, as he declared, "I've never seen anyone more beautiful." Savanah's breath hitched with his words, and she let out a breathy sigh as he reached for her hand, guiding her onto the bed next to him. "I love you, Savanah, so very much." She caressed his cheek and brought her lips to his, at first gentle and timid, then deepened their kiss, their mouths opening, their tongues coaxing and exploring. Breaking their kiss, Rami rose from the bed while Savanah lifted onto her elbows to watch him. He reached for the towel and slowly, seductively unwrapped it from his body.

SAVANAH'S EYES dilated as she took in Rami in all his magnificent, naked glory. He was tanned, lean, and muscular, every ridge and contour perfection. Then she let her eyes daringly travel lower to his hard steel length, smooth and powerful. She swallowed, not having seen a naked man before. His body reminded her of the Rodin sculpture, The Thinker, with lean, sinewy muscles. *He's beautiful.*

She shimmied into the middle of the bed, her head resting on the pillows as he crawled onto the bed and lay down next to her. They stared into each other's eyes for a while, relishing this moment with them lying here together, naked and vulnerable. Rami reached up, smoothing back her hair, his eyes soft and sensual as he brought his lips to hers in a passionate kiss, his tongue tangling with hers as he pulled her flush with his hard and ready body. All nervousness dissipated as she ran her hands over his taut back and down to his behind, gripping and pulling him closer to her, his hard length pressing into her belly. He rolled on top of her, and her legs spread open, making room for his body at her juncture. She kissed him hungrily, her desire for him building at a frantic pace. Her pelvis instinctively rose off the mattress to press against him as the wet softness of her silken folds slid against his hard length.

"Mi Amor, I need to get protection," he panted against her lips. Pulling away, he crawled off the bed and reached into his jeans on the floor, then climbed back onto the bed, kneeling, her legs open to him. He gazed upon her rosy center, wet and ready, and groaned in appreciation. Rami ripped open the condom and rolled it on, then settled between her legs again.

"I'm going to go slow because I don't want to hurt you," he reassured, meeting her lustful gaze as he glanced down, positioning himself at her entrance. She nodded as he pushed forward, his length sliding into her body slowly, the feel of him filling her, new and causing her internal muscles to clench around his length, drawing him deeper. She met his cloudy gaze, the look on his face one of reverence as he asked, "Are you okay?"

"I'm okay," she managed, her body pulsing with new sensation. "Keep going."

He continued to sink into her, a barrier of resistance giving way, a stab of pain radiating through her core, causing an inadvertent gasp to escape her lips. Rami searched her eyes, and she breathed out a long breath and reached up, smoothing down the creases between his concerned brows. "I'm fine, Rami. I promise." He pulled back slightly and pressed further, making her moan this time in pleasure. "That felt good," she cried as he did it again, this time taking her deeper yet. Rami set a slow and steady cadence, her body opening more with each press and pull of his hips.

"Oh, my God, Savanah, you feel amazing. So hot

around me and so tight." His voice was thick with pleasure as he rocked himself into her. She met him with each grind and press, her body melting into his as he kept his pace.

"Kiss me," she begged on a gasp as his lips found hers and his tongue slid against hers. With the tease of his tongue, she pulled her mouth away, their eyes meeting as her body tightened around him, and she moaned, her eyes closing in sweet ecstasy.

A WHITE-HOT HEAT climbed up Rami's spine as stars formed behind his eyes, his body releasing along with her gripping spasms. A long feral groan escaped from his lips as his body gave into the sheer unbridled pleasure. By the time his vision cleared he looked down on Savanah whose face was flushed a rosy pink, her gorgeous blue eyes overcast with satisfaction, and a satiated grin curved her kiss bitten lips. Overcome with bliss, love and gratitude, Rami leaned down, kissing her mouth, her cheeks, her neck, her forehead, painting kisses all over her, making her squirm and giggle under his hard, heavy body.

He rolled to the side and off the bed, excusing himself to the ensuite to dispose of the condom. She followed using the bathroom, then returned to him under the covers. As she climbed in next to him, curling her long, lean naked body around his and nestled her head on his chest, Rami wondered if it would always be like this. A perfect torrent of love, lust, and unbridled passion. They lay there a long time in contemplative silence before Rami broke their revelry by deadpanning, "Five out of five stars, would definitely recommend."

Savanah broke into a giggle, feathering her fingers through the curls that kissed his neck as she closed her eyes, him following suit and they drifted off into a blissfully satiated slumber.

CHAPTER 7

The morning came, bands of light dancing across the wall from the slits of her bedroom blinds. Rami's eyes peeled open to the sweet cotton candy cascade of Savanah's hair fanned out on her pillowcase. She was facing away, but the heat of her body radiated across the space between them. Both still naked, he slid his body closer, his arm curling around her waist, pulling her into him. The curve of her body fit like a puzzle piece against his. Rami buried his face in her hair, inhaling deeply. The sweet smell of her skin was intoxicating. She stirred a moment, letting out a little whimper, then her breathing steadied again as she remained fast asleep. He lay there a long time, his hand splayed on her stomach, taking in the warmth of her body and thinking about last night. *Last night was perfect.* Flashbacks of the feel of her under him and how their bodies fit together so seam-lessly, making his pulse quicken and body harden. He wanted so much more with Savanah, both physically and emotionally. She was his first crush, his first kiss, his first

"

and only lover. He couldn't help but think, *this is just the beginning for us.*

Savanah let out a little moan and squirmed in his hold, her hand finding his and threading with his fingers on her stomach. She sighed contentedly. *I love her.*

"Good morning, Mi amor," he said, trailing kisses from her shoulder up her neck to her ear and back down again.

Savanah wiggled away from him and giggled, so he pulled her flush with him again. She let out a little "Oh", as his hard arousal made itself known.

"Sorry." Rami apologized with a groan. "You're just so sexy; my body has a mind of its own."

"I don't mind." She replied, rubbing her backside against his hardness.

Rami groaned, pulling her hips firmly against his body, creating friction. She reached behind her and boldly gripped him with her hand, running up and down, making a low growl rumble from his chest. "Savanah, I need to be in you again," he said roughly. "But I don't have any more protection with me."

Savanah let him go and leaned over, reaching down to her bedside table, the sound of a drawer opening. She turned to look at him and held up a box of condoms.

An incredulous laugh burst forth from Rami's lips as he asked, "You have condoms?"

She grinned, her eyes dancing as she replied, "I bought some this week, thinking we may need them soon. I wanted to be prepared."

He groaned, cupping her chin, bringing her lips to his. "I love you so much. Do you know that?"

She giggled, opening the box and handing him a foil

packet. He ripped open the package and eagerly sheathed himself. She hitched her hip over his, both still lying back to front. With her open to him, Rami lined himself up and sank into her, the heat of her inviting him in completely. "Oh, God." she cried out as he gripped her hips, sliding in and out of her body leisurely and languidly, claiming her. They made love like this for a while, enjoying the slow steady rhythm and savoring their newfound connection. Rami could feel his body needing more, so he slid the blanket off them and said, "Go on your hands and knees."

Savanah shifted her body until she was on her hands and knees, and he positioned himself behind her. He sank into her again, this time deeper, making them both gasp from the sensation. He smoothed his hands over her spine, lowering her head to the pillow as he dug into her hips and quickened his pace. She moaned with each thrust; the guttural sounds she was making fueled him to keep his momentum. The now familiar burn ignited low in his core, crawling quickly up his spine. Her cries of pleasure muffled by the pillow; her walls gripped him as waves of pleasure rippled through her body, stimulating his own release. Tumbling over the edge together, Rami let out a moan of his own as he lifted her body, bringing her back to his chest in a tight hold as he called her name. She laid her head back on his shoulder as tremors surged through their bodies and their chests heaved breathlessly.

"I love you Rami," she panted; their bodies still connected. "I know now that I was waiting for you."

He kissed her cheek and held her, the sheen of sweat on their bodies glistening in the dim light of her room. *I had been waiting for you, too.*

* * *

"I LOVE THAT YOU CAN COOK." Savanah said, watching Rami mix a combination of chopped spinach, canned artichokes, and mayonnaise together, then scoop it onto large pieces of crusty bread.

"You're the one who had these ingredients in your cupboards and fridge," he said, sprinkling cheese on each slice and turning to pop them into the oven.

"Ingredients I'm good at. What to make with them? I am not." She said, taking a sip of her hot tea and curling her fingers around the lapel of her terry robe.

They hadn't gotten dressed or ready for the day yet despite the noon hour, enjoying a lazy morning in naked exploration, with neither wanting to break their euphoric love bubble.

Rami rounded the island and stood in front of her, his tanned skin gorgeous in the midday light. She raked her eyes over him, appreciating how comfortable he was walking around in his boxers in her house. Taking in his lean, sexy body, she glanced up at him through her thick lashes, her hands running over the sides of his torso.

"With that look you give me, I may never want to leave this house," he said, meeting her gaze. "Will you come with me to family dinner again tonight?"

Savanah replied, pulling him into her, kissing his stomach. "Yes, I will, but let me check my phone to double check if I have anything going on today." She hopped off her stool, quickly found her phone in her jacket pocket and swiped it open, seeing a text from Dee.

Dee: Girl, I better get the tea on what happened last night.

No deets if you don't want to, but this friend is curious! FYI check out this link if you want to relive last night.

"Dee uploaded a video from last night's performance on YouTube." Savanah told Rami as she came around the island standing next to him. Savanah clicked the link, and the video started with Savanah being led to the stage, his profession of love, and going into his serenade.

Rami looked at the 320,000 views and his eyes widened as he asked, "When did she upload this?"

Savanah clicked a few times and replied, "Looks like a few hours ago."

Rami ran his hands through his hair, and he started to pace. "That's a lot of views, isn't it?"

"Yeah, I don't know the standards on this, but it seems like a lot," she said, now scrolling through the comments. "Woah!" she said, bringing the phone closer, her eyes widening as she stared at the screen. "There's a comment here from… Rami, you need to read this!"

Rami grabbed her phone and looked, his eyes bugged out as he exclaimed, "Holy fuck!" He started laughing almost manically, pacing the length of her kitchen and running his hand through his dark curls as he read the comment from Coldplay's frontman. "Great rendition. Someone needs to sign these guys!"

"Holy crap! Rami, this is real! There are thousands of comments here!" she added.

They spent the afternoon scrolling through comment after comment, watching the views increase at a rapid pace. Many asked where they could stream their music. So many comments on him specifically and about Savanah. They laughed at all the fire and heart emojis. Of course, with the good, you got the odd troll, but they paid them no mind, as most were positive and supportive.

"Looks like Layne set up the channel last night and uploaded the video, as well as a few more from the concert." Savanah said, looking up at Rami's overwhelmed stare. "Dee must have helped them. Looks like they uploaded five videos between last night and this morning."

Rami shook his head, his smile permanently painted on his face as he combed his hand through his hair again, disbelief clouding his gaze. "I can't believe this is happening."

Savanah wrapped her arms around his waist and hugged him tightly as she met his gaze. "You deserve this Rami."

Rami turned his attention to her, his eyes so soft and loving, as he turned, taking her face in his hands, "Thank you," he said, planting a passionate kiss on her lips as he lifted her to straddle his body. "We have some time before we need to get ready for dinner," he said, breaking their kiss, lifting her and carrying her towards the bedroom.

"Well then, Mr. Rockstar, you better rock my world."

* * *

THE NEXT FEW weeks were a whirlwind for Prairie Sound. Their notoriety increased with video shares, the views skyrocketing. By the following week they found them-selves being interviewed for newspapers, radio stations and TV Stations and fielding calls from agents wanting to sign them. By the end of October, they were no longer just a well-known local band. They had gained national status, and their popularity was growing every day. They had signed with an agent who was now working with them to secure a record deal.

Despite the craziness that now surrounded the band, Rami and Savanah found tidbits of time to spend with each other. In fact, most weekends when Prairie Sound wasn't playing gigs, they spent their time wrapped around each other in bed. The newfound intimacy between them, becoming familiar.

"I feel like I could stay like this forever." Savanah sighed, resting her head on Rami's chest, her long leg curled around his body. Rami kissed her head and stroked her hair with tender affection. "Do you think Prairie Sound will be picked up by a label soon?" she asked, turning to meet his gaze.

"I think so. We have enough original songs for our first album and our agent says once we get signed, we will probably have singles released on streaming services, but we'll also be working in the studio to record."

"Are you excited?" she asked, her eyes brightening.

"Of course," he laughed. "But it's also a little over-whelming and surreal. I still feel like I need to pinch myself, you know."

Savanah gave him a playful pinch on his side, and he tickled her, making her giggle and squirm under his touch. He rolled on top of her, hovering over her body, the heat of his skin scorching and melting her into the mattress. His eyes searching hers, a look of seriousness, washing over his face as he said, "Savanah, I don't know what's going to happen with the band and all this exposure, but I want you to know that you're important to me. I'm always going to be your Rami."

Savanah searched his eyes, his declaration speaking both to her heart and her head. The thought of how fame and notoriety could change him and their relationship had crossed her mind. *How would it work if he was gone for long periods of time?* Right now, it was getting more and more difficult to find time for each other. *Would we be able to make it work?* All these thoughts and more weighed heavily on her heart.

* * *

SAVANAH PULLED into Garrett and Bea's driveway and glanced in the rearview mirror at the house across the street. The driveway was full, and she immediately noticed Rami's little sports car. She knew Prairie Sound was having a writing session today at his house and they would be at it all day. She sighed a long-drawn-out sigh. It had been almost two weeks since they last spent time together and the desire to see Rami was almost over-whelming, yet she knew she needed to give him space right now, to let him process all the craziness surrounding the band and not pull him away from their creative process.

She got out of her vehicle and approached Garrett and Bea's door. With her mind a jumble of conflicting emotions, she was never happier for the distraction of spending time with three of her favorite people and with the task of helping plan Garrett and Bea's upcoming wedding.

The door flung open, and Amelia greeted her as she always did, with a barrage of hugs and kisses. She entered the kitchen, where Garrett and Bea were settled at the kitchen table, mugs of coffee in hand. Bea got up to give her a hug and get her a cup of coffee. Savanah sat down at the table, setting down the binder of ideas and information she put together for them, and looked up to meet her brother's gaze.

"You look like you have the weight of the world on you today," he said, his smile turning to a concerned frown. "Something bothering you?"

Emotion rose high in her chest from his question, but she feigned a smile and let out a long exhale to disguise her emotions. "No, just got a lot of stuff going on. It's all good," she replied, giving Garrett a reassuring look.

He took a sip of his coffee, his eyes still analyzing her, and she knew he could read her like a book. She also knew he wasn't going to make her open to him if she wasn't ready to.

Bea handed her a coffee and took a seat next to Garrett as Savanah went into professional mode and they reviewed their wedding plans.

"Alright! I think all the important stuff for the wedding have been decided on. The ceremony location, the reception location, the flowers etc. I'll see what I can curate for you, Bea regarding a dress, as I know exactly what you're looking for." Savanah added with a wink. "Now, do you want a DJ or a band for the reception?"

"Honestly, I was hoping Prairie Sound would play for the wedding, but who knows if they'll be available." Bea replied. "With them going viral and blowing up, Marnie told me a tour is definitely possible in the coming year."

"I think if I speak to the band about it now, they can decide to be available at that time. Marnie is right, though. So much is up in the air right now and it's hard to tell what things will look like for them in July. There is also the factor that they've signed with an agent, so I'm not sure of the protocol. I think they have a say in what they take on and what they don't take on, though, so I'll ask Rami."

"You and Rami are officially a couple, I presume," Bea asked curiously. "At least the entire world knows how you feel about each other."

Savanah smiled and her cheeks went rosy thinking about how his first 'I love you' to her was painted all over the internet for anyone to see. "Yes, I guess anonymity is not something we have at the moment."

"Are you okay with that?" Garrett asked, furrowing his brows in concern. "I know you left modeling because you couldn't deal with the lifestyle and didn't enjoy the spotlight. I would imagine if Rami and his band hit it big, it would become intense. Like what you went through before, but on a bigger scale."

Am I okay with all of this? Do I want to be part of that scene? Do I want to constantly be in the spotlight or under public scrutiny of others? Do I want to give up my quiet existence? The worry and the whirling thoughts made her chest tighten and throat constrict. She didn't want to have to deal with all of that and be thrown back into that world, but she loved Rami and being his girlfriend meant she would have to sacrifice some of her carefully cultivated peace. *Am I willing to do that for him?* There was only one way to reply.

"I've thought about it, and right now, I'm just taking it one day at a time." She answered honestly. "Rami is so talented, and I'm not going to hold him back. This is his dream and because I love him, I guess we'll just have to see where it takes him and his band."

"He's pretty lucky to have you, Savanah." Bea added, reaching over and touching her hand, sincerity in her gaze. "He's a truly good guy and comes from a good family. I think you two will figure it out."

But would they?

The fall grew colder, and the inevitable winter snow arrived, blanketing everything in a layer of wet, heavy snow. With Christmas three weeks away, the hustle had started, and Savanah found herself swamped at work with customers and countless requests for her to find them the perfect outfits for the holidays.

On top of spending long days at the boutique, she was struggling to navigate time to see Rami. Spending most of his time, either writing songs, performing with his band, or now working on their first album in the studio, they would text daily, but some days, the texts were short and clipped because of their busy schedules. She tried to stay supportive and take the crumbs of his time he could give her, but she had to admit it was becoming excruciatingly difficult. She craved being around him and missed him with an all-consuming ache that physically hurt. She found her emotions were shaky, and she yearned for the feel of his warm body curled around hers at night. She wasn't sure what she was going to do, but she needed to talk to him and let him know how she was feeling.

Savanah snuggled up on the couch with a book, a bowl of popcorn and a glass of wine, feeling sleepy and exhausted from a full day at her boutique. She started to read, but soon found herself dozing on the couch when her doorbell startled her awake. Groggily, she pulled her robe tight over her body as she made her way down the stairs to her front entrance. She peered through the peephole and her face immediately brightened. *Rami.* Opening the door, she leapt into Rami's arms, curling her body around his. He laughed deeply as she planted a kiss on his lips, and she threaded her fingers through his soft, curly hair.

Carrying her into the house and locking the door behind him, he pulled his lips away from hers and met her eyes as he commented, "Somebody missed me."

"I've missed you so much." Savanah confessed, her voice edging with the longing she had been feeling. "What are you doing here? I thought you and the guys were going to be in the studio late tonight."

He set her down on the floor and cupped her face in his hands, looking deep into her eyes. "I told them I needed to go see my girlfriend," he said simply. "It's been 3 weeks since I've seen you, and texting isn't enough for me. I needed to see your beautiful face."

Savanah smiled as she leaned in to kiss him. He tasted like mint and the scent of his sandalwood cologne enveloped her like a warm, soothing hug. *God, I missed him.* She teased his upper lip with her tongue. Rami opened to her, his tongue sliding alongside hers, their kiss deepening as the desire between them became urgent, their mouths seeking more. He carried her up the stairs to the main floor and over to the couch, taking a seat with her straddling his hips. His hands tangled in her hair and skated over her neck and shoulders, sliding her terry robe down her arms. He pulled the side of her button-down pajama top down to reveal her bare shoulder as he kissed and licked the tender flesh beneath.

Savanah moaned, her core pulsing with need as he unbuttoned her top and let it fall from her shoulders to the floor with her robe. Her breasts bare to his perusal and touch, he brought one rosy peak into his mouth, sucking as he teased the other with his thumb.

"That feels amazing." she panted, lost in the sensation of his fevered attention.

He let her nipple go and looked into her eyes, now dark and hooded with desire. "There is something I've been wanting to try with you."

"What's that?" she asked breathlessly.

"I want to taste you here," he said, slipping his hand into her sleeping shorts, running his fingers through her soft wet folds.

She moaned at his words and touch as he strummed her like his guitar, circling her pleasure point, and their wanton gazes met. "We've never done that."

"I thought maybe we could add it to the playlist." He replied, his voice gravely and so impossibly sexy. "Climb off me and lie down."

She climbed off his lap, and he rose from the couch, straightening out throw pillows to support her head. She lay down angled toward him, and he kneeled next to the couch. Curling his fingers around the waistband of her sleeping shorts and panties, he slowly dragged them down her long legs and off. Spreading her wide, the cool air drifted over her wet core. Savanah had never been so exposed or aroused in her life, watching Rami take in her most intimate part. His eyes met hers. "You are so beautiful," he murmured, his hot breath cascading over the sensitive flesh. "Tell me if this feels good, okay?"

She nodded, trying hard to breathe as he lowered his head and ran his tongue along her seam. Her breath caught, and hands fisted the pillows as he repeated the move, running his tongue over the length of her apex and teasing at the bundle of nerves at her center.

"Rami." she gasped, as he lifted his head and met her gaze, his eyes dark as midnight.

"More?" he asked with a sexy smirk.

"Yes."

Feverishly, he pleased her as she shamelessly writhed and rocked against his mouth, her hips lifting off the couch, and fingers gripping tight to his hair. Lost in the new sensations, her climax teetering on the edge, she threw her head back and cried. "Rami, I'm..." Her words caught in her throat as a wave of pleasure overtook her and her body shuddered. He didn't relent, helping her reach the pinnacle and slowly come down from the high. Savanah covered her eyes, her cheeks flushed warm and her breathing ragged.

"Was that good?" he asked, his lips and chin glistening from her arousal.

"So good," she managed, removing her hand from her eyes to see a look of utter accomplishment on his face.

"Kiss me," she demanded, aroused by the thought of tasting herself on his lips. He climbed onto her, his body hovering over hers as he kissed her, the salty, sweet musky taste of her climax making her libido go into overdrive. He rose to his feet and started to undress, removing each article of clothing. His wanton eyes locked on hers. She sat up watching him, as he slid his briefs down his legs, letting his hard length spring free. She reached for him, taking him in hand to stroke him, his head falling back with a groan. She marveled at how his member pulsed with her touch, and her mouth salivated at the thought of tasting him too. "Can I taste you?" she asked, staring up at him, the desire to have him at her mercy, heady.

His dark lustful eyes looked down on her as a strangled 'yes' tumbled from his lips. Savanah urged him to sit down on the couch, as she pinned him with her sensual gaze, ran her hands over his pecs and down the ridges of his torso, back to his manhood, curling her fingers around his girth and stroking. He let out a husky growl, clutched at the couch and all his muscles tensed in anticipation as she lowered her head, taking her first taste. Rami closed his eyes with pleasure as she took the length of him into her mouth, creating a suction as she flattened her tongue and teased the underside. He let out a long loud growl and involuntarily bucked his hips off the couch, causing him to hit the back of her throat. His eyes flew open at this as she drew her head back up and circled the crown with her tongue.

"Oh, my God, sorry, that was insane," he managed. Savanah let him go, meeting his eyes, a coquettish grin on her face as she lowered her mouth and took him in again, repeating the move. He tried to control the need to pump into her mouth as she sucked him in deeper. "Holy fuck!" he cried out as she hummed around his member, bringing him closer to his release. "I need to feel all of you!" She lifted her head, letting him go with a pop as she rose to her feet. "My jeans, my wallet, I have a condom in there," he said roughly, his voice dripping with desire.

She pulled out his wallet and opened it. Finding one tucked into an inner pocket, she handed it to him as he ripped it open and slid it down his length. He gazed up at her, his eyes blazing with want as he put his hand out for her to climb onto him, straddling his hips. He positioned himself at her entrance as she sank onto the length of him, taking every inch he had to offer. They both sighed at the feeling of their coupling, now craved and deliciously familiar. She moved over him, with a slow steady pace, their eyes locked on each other as their breaths mingled hot and heady. He gripped her behind, pulling, pushing, the erotic grind of her hips causing him to dig his fingers into her soft, subtle flesh. Lost in pleasure, she threw her head back, and he brought the peak of a breast in his mouth, sucking hard. She cried out as her body clenched around him, gripping him like a vice, her climax taking over. Through her shudders of pleasure, he moved her over him, chasing his own release as he followed her over the edge. She collapsed on him, burying her face in his shoulder. Their bodies joined as they held onto each other, their chests heaving with shattered breaths. "I missed you so much." she rasped against his skin, all her emotions coming out in a flood of salty tears. He held onto her tightly as she cried into his shoulder, and he rubbed her back to soothe her. She lifted her tear-streaked face to meet his gaze, his eyes glistening with emotion too as he kissed her wet cheeks. "Mi amor, I won't let it go that long again. I promise."

* * *

RAMI MADE good on his promise to spend more time with Savanah, carving out time between his studio sessions so they could be together. Now, with the holiday season upon them, both were ready to enjoy their first Christmas together as a couple.

"Baby, why did you insist on such a big tree?" she giggled as she took in the large Douglas Fir scraping her ceiling.

He rose to his feet and took in the tree; it was tall and wide and far too big for her small space. He just shook his head and laughed too. "All I can say is this is the first tree I've bought and, well, I think I got a little overzealous."

"You think?" she giggled, looking at the peak bending to accommodate the height of the tree.

He just laughed and put his arm around her, pulling her into him. "Hey, it's our first Christmas together. Go big or go home!"

Savanah slapped his chest playfully and shook her head. "Let me pull out the decorations. No way am I hauling that beast out of here now."

"Don't be calling Dougie, here a beast," he said pretending to pet the tree. "It's okay, boy, she'll grow to love you."

"You are nuts!" she giggled as she pulled a large tote of decorations out of her hallway storage closet and carried them into the living room.

She opened the tote and Rami joined her, reaching in to pick up a handmade ornament with a picture of her much younger self in the middle.

"I remember this!" he exclaimed; his smile wide. "Didn't we make these at Camp Clearwater?" She nodded, looking at the ornament in his hand. "How old were you in this picture?"

"Nine." she replied. "That was my first year at Camp."

"The year we met," he said with a nostalgic smile as he took in the pretty blonde girl with big expressive blue eyes in the picture. "I remember the first time I saw you so vividly, too. You were standing in line, waiting to find out what bunkhouse you were in. You looked so shy and scared, like you may cry at any second. I remember going up to you because I didn't like seeing you so sad. When I said hello to you, you looked at me and you smiled the sweetest smile I had ever seen, and your big blue eyes went from so sad to literally sparkling in the sunshine. I just remember thinking you were an angel and feeling so happy to stand next to you."

Savanah reached up and touched his face tenderly. "I remember I was so anxious, as it was my first sleep-away camp and all I wanted to do was go home. Then this friendly, tanned, dark-haired skinny boy sidled up to me and said hello. I remember looking up and seeing your chocolate brown eyes and feeling like I was going to be okay, and that I was safe. I'll never forget that moment. I felt like I had a friend."

Rami looked down at her, his emotions and memories hovering on the surface. "Savanah, I still see you as my friend. My best friend."

"I see you that way too," she replied, her eyes glossy with tears. "So many times, when we're together, laughing and having fun, it reminds me of all those summers at Camp Clearwater and how my favorite part of camp was always you."

Rami pulled her in for a hug and kissed her head sweetly, letting out a long exhale, "Those are some of my favorite memories too," he agreed as he held her tight. They stood there wrapped up together for a long time, both of their eyes drifting over to the gigantic tree taking over her living room. Savanah buried her face in his chest, her shoulders shaking with a giggle, and Rami burst out laughing too as he conceded, "Next year, you pick out the tree."

* * *

RAMI and the rest of the band took the week of Christmas off. This meant that Christmas week was full of family, friends, and lots and lots of food. One thing Savanah was quickly realizing is everything the Perez family did revolved around incredible food. With their nightly Navidad celebrations, you could always guarantee you would come away with a full belly and a full heart.

Christmas also brought another milestone for Rami and Savanah's relationship; Rami was going to meet her parents for the first time. Although they may have met him when dropping Savanah off at camp when they were kids, they hadn't met him as an adult and not as Savanah's boyfriend.

"Are you nervous about meeting my parents?" Savanah asked, taking Rami's hand as they walked up to Garrett and Bea's house.

"No, but do I need to be?" he asked with a laugh and a squeeze of his hand. "You've asked me five times now if I'm nervous."

Savanah gave him a sheepish look. "Sorry, maybe I'm the one that's nervous. I've never introduced them to a boyfriend before!"

Rami stopped, and she turned to face him as he wrapped his arms around her, saying confidently. "It's going to be fine."

She let out a long exhale and nodded as they strode to the front door. Amelia opened the door and squealed when she saw Rami.

"Hey, there beautiful! Merry Christmas!" Rami exclaimed as Amelia jumped into his arms, making him drop the presents he was holding.

"Hey, what about me?" she asked, feigning insult.

Amelia rolled her eyes, which had become a new thing in her sassy repertoire, and let go of Rami to go give her aunt a hug.

Bea came around the corner, seeing all the gifts strewn about the front entrance. "Oh, my goodness! Amelia, can you pick these up and put them under the tree?" Amelia let go of Savanah and nodded while Bea greeted them. "Merry Christmas you two! We're ready for lunch, and you are the last to arrive."

They both removed their outerwear and followed Bea

into the kitchen, where everyone was milling around the kitchen island.

"Savanah!" Her mother greeted her with a big hug. "Merry Christmas!" She turned her attention to Rami and took him in a moment as a smile of recognition swept across her face. "I remember you as a little boy when I dropped Savanah off at Camp. Ramiro, you have grown into such a handsome young man. Merry Christmas!"

"Nice to meet you again, Mrs. Smithfield." Rami replied, leaning down to accept her hug and giving her a kiss on the cheek.

"Oh, please call me Lisa." she said, her face blooming with a rosy hue as she beamed at Rami. Savanah looked at her mother and shook her head. *Even my mother can't escape his charms.*

"We haven't had a chance to meet yet." Her father stepped forward, putting his hand out to Rami. "Bryan Smithfield." Rami accepted his hand in a firm shake. "Please call me Bryan."

"Nice to meet you, Bryan." Rami replied in greeting.

Garrett and Rami gave each other a brotherly hug, and everyone gathered around the table, finding their seats. As they enjoyed their Irish meal of glazed baked ham, potatoes, roasted carrots and turnips, along with Marnie's Irish Soda Bread, the conversation went to Garrett and Bea's upcoming wedding.

"Savanah, did you ask Rami if Prairie Sound was available to play at the reception?" Bea asked curiously.

Rami turned to Savanah, and she winced. "Sorry, I haven't asked yet. Honestly, it's been so busy and between the shop and everything that Rami has had going on lately, it completely slipped my mind."

Rami set his hand on Savanah's to reassure her, and he turned his attention to Garrett and Bea. "What's the date of the wedding? I can speak to the band and see what we can figure out. We are booked out for about 5 months, right now, but if it's in summer, we may be free. And of course, if we get picked up by a tour, that may play a factor in our availability."

"The wedding is July 17th." Garrett replied. "We just thought it would be awesome to have a live band and, of course, you guys are the best."

"Can I let you know this week?" Rami asked.

They both nodded.

"You're a musician?" Lisa asked, her eyes wide with curiosity. "What sort of music do you play?"

"Yes, I am. We're an alternative rock band mostly, but we do a lot of covers of classic rock songs, too. Right now, however, we're working on our first album that is all our own original music."

"They've been a band for almost eight years but recently they went viral," Savanah added proudly.

"Viral?" Bryan asks for clarification.

"It's when a video is posted and becomes extremely popular, causing it to spread across the internet and over social media platforms. In this case, they've gone viral on YouTube and that video has been shared across all different social media apps," Garrett explained. "Their one video alone, last I looked, has millions of views."

"Our one YouTube video has funded our entire album

and likely will fund any travel costs for the band over the next year." Rami added.

"Wow, that's impressive!" Bea exclaimed. "I had no idea that you got paid for your content."

"Neither did I," Rami replied with a laugh. "As a band, we were never into social media and other than for advertising shows, we really didn't realize how it could impact our band's exposure. Then Savanah introduced us to Dee and between her and my bandmates, they developed a plan and well, the rest is history, I guess."

"Oh, that Dee is such a smart cookie!" Lisa exclaimed. "Well, it sounds like you and your band are on your way to something big."

"We think this could be the catalyst to more for sure. It has put a big spotlight on us. We now have an agent, and the next goal is to release our first album, acquire a record deal and fingers crossed, join a major tour. Maybe opening for a well-known band or singer."

"Then that would likely mean months away on tour?" Bryan asked, his face serious as his eyes flitted to Savanah.

"Possibly. It's hard to say exactly." Rami replied honestly. "It could be a few shows or an entire leg of a tour."

Savanah's dad looked at her with a dubious expression on his face. She didn't miss the concern in his eyes, and she swallowed down hard. She knew what her father was thinking. *You left your rising career in the modeling world because of the inability to handle the spotlight and now you're willingly throwing yourself back in the spotlight as the girlfriend of a popular musician.* Savanah was well aware of the irony of the situation and that her father was feeling wary about this. Savanah broke her father's gaze and glanced down at her hands, which she was now wringing anxiously, as an awkward quiet fell around the table.

Bea, noticing the shift in mood and her anxious tell, met her gaze with support and got up from the table gathering plates as she asked, "How about we open some presents?"

Everyone got up at once and she gave Savanah a passing glance, followed by a wink. Savanah was never more thankful for Bea's quick thinking and ability to read a room.

CHAPTER 9

With Prairie Sound's popularity continuing to grow, they were booked to headline an iconic Winnipeg hot spot for New Years Eve. The well-known location was an old theatre transformed into a concert venue and it was where many local bands were discovered. In fact, according to the band's agent, several representatives from record labels and tours were rumored to be in the crowd tonight, so Prairie Sound was ditching the covers and their setlist was all new material for the first time. A debut of sorts for their upcoming album.

"We'll start with Go My Direction and end with Deeper Meaning." Rami reminded his bandmates, and they all nodded in agreement.

"Hey, are Savanah and Dee going to be in the audience tonight?" Steve asked as he flopped onto the dressing room couch.

"They're planning on it." Rami replied, taking a seat on a stool.

"Man, that Dee still won't go out with me! I've been asking and asking, but she keeps turning me down!" Rex exclaimed with exasperation. "I keep telling her that once you go blue, you'll never be through." he added, running his hands over the sides of his blue mohawk.

"I think that's your problem, Rex." Layne commented, giving him a playful punch in the arm. "You come on too strong."

Rex gave him a scowl, clutching his arm and feigning injury. "Hey, don't damage the arm. It's my money maker!"

"Can you guys cut it out?" Rami asked, flashing them a glare before he started to pace. "Tonight is a big deal. So many of the hottest Manitoba bands have played this venue, and many have been discovered right here."

Steve rose from the couch and put his hand on Rami's shoulder. "The guys are just letting off some steam. We all promise you; we understand how big of a deal this is, and we got you, man."

"Yeah, we got you!" Rex exclaimed, holding his drumsticks in the air. "We're going to rock this place tonight!"

The door opened and the stage director peered in. "Are you ready to get the show started?"

Rami nodded and glanced between his bandmates, determination flashing in his eyes. "Let's do this!"

"THIS PLACE IS AWESOME!" Savanah exclaimed to Dee as they made their way into the venue space. The venue was large with high ceilings typical of theatres, with limited seating around the bar areas and at one end of the room were intimate nooks to steal away. The rest was an open space with a huge stage set up at the opposite end, allowing for rush seating for the concert. Despite the ample space, it was packed with people milling about, and Savanah could already feel a bead of sweat on her brow from so many bodies packed into the space.

"Let's grab a drink and wait for the show to start." Dee suggested. "Do you want to get close to the stage or hang back for the show?"

"Hang back, maybe." Savanah replied, surveying the crowd with apprehension. "I don't want to get crushed by this crowd."

Dee nodded in agreement, and they made their way to the bar, Dee placed them each a drink order and once their drinks were in hand, they found a spot off to the side where they could see the stage, but the crowd wasn't as pressed.

Savanah glanced around, feeling awkward, an unexpected discomfort taking over. Where they stood, she noticed a group of people pointing towards them and their heads leaned in together in muffled murmurs with their eyes on her. *Were they talking about her? Did they recognize her from the viral video?* Her heart pounded nervously, and her anxiety started to rise at the thought.

"You seem off tonight." Dee observed, turning to her friend, her brows knit together in concern. "Is something bothering you?"

Savanah's eyes went downcast, as unexpected emotion hovered close to the surface and tightened her throat. *Where was all this emotion coming from?* Ever since

Christmas Day when Rami met her parents, she had been in her head. She and Rami were able to spend most of the holidays together, but after the noticeable concern from her dad, she couldn't help but return to the conversation around that dinner table, and the wary look on her father's face. She had left a lifestyle in the spotlight behind. She had made it clear to her family that she wanted nothing to do with the loss of privacy, public scrutiny and not to mention everything that goes on behind the scenes or behind closed doors. Although she was young when she started modeling and she had a guardian with her at the beginning, with her parents overseeing her budding career, once she turned 18, she was almost primarily on her own. What she saw in those few years was way more than any young woman should be exposed to. In fact, Savanah had almost been pulled into the glitz and glamour with the dark shadows hovering on the edges herself. Seeing other girls, many of which were her friends, pulled into the deep depths of depravity and unable to find their light again. Savanah wasn't about to let this quiet, peaceful life she had created for herself be completely upended. *How can I be with Rami and still maintain this quiet, calm life I worked so hard to create for myself?* This question kept running through her head on repeat. That worry, combined with her resurfacing insecurities, were affecting her far more than she initially realized.

"Yeah, sorry, just got a lot on my mind tonight." Savanah replied, feigning a smile and trying to keep the emotion from overflowing. From the look on Dee's face, she wasn't fooled.

"If you want to talk about it, you know you can open up to me," Dee reminded, as she looped her arm in hers and met her gaze with compassion. "I'm a great listener."

Savanah met her friend's concerned gaze with appreciation. Dee had her brush with fame as well when she was younger, having been in several national commercials as a child, and being part of the theatre community for years. If anyone could understand how she was feeling right now, it would be Dee.

"Hey, that's the girl from the video." Savanah overheard a woman say not far from where there were standing. "She's not so hot. What does he even see in her?"

Dee, hearing the woman as well, pulled away from Savanah to give this girl a piece of her mind and Savanah gripped her arm harder to stop her from a confrontation. She met Dee's fiery gaze imploring her to ignore the comment. Savanah had already had some trolls post negative comments on their video. She knew reading these comments was a bad idea, but curiosity had gotten the better of her. The harsh commentary and unkind words stung and reminded her of the criticism she received while modeling. She knew how cruel people could be, especially keyboard warriors.

"It's not worth it." Savanah said to her friend.

Dee straightened up and caught the woman's eye, giving her a nasty glare, making the woman recoil and move to a different area with her friends. Savanah appreciated Dee's desire to protect her and was grateful that she always had her back.

The lights came down, signaling the concert was about

to start and the cheers erupted, bouncing off the walls of the large space. Electricity entered the room as it always did when the spotlight zoned in on Rami, his electric guitar in hand as he shredded it, and as the stage lights came up, his bandmates appeared behind him. Every time Savanah saw him perform, she was in awe of the power he wielded on stage. *My Rami. Was he still hers?* A feeling of doubt creeping in with the question. Yes, he was her boyfriend; she loved him, and he loved her but now that their fandom was building, she could feel the cosmic shift. He belonged to everyone in this room, all his fans, all the people that watched his videos and felt the same electricity she was feeling right now watching him. The realization of this caused an uneasiness in the pit of her stomach and a slow burning ache painfully gripped her heart.

With another incredible show in the books and adrenaline still pumping through Rami's body, he clapped his bandmates on the back. There was nothing like the electricity of a sold-out crowd and tonight the energy was surging.

"Fuck, that concert was killer." Rex growled, flopping down on the couch in their dressing room.

"Agreed! Honestly, I don't think it could have gone any better." Layne added.

"The acoustics are stellar in this venue." Steve commented as his excited gaze flitted between his band-mates. "Can you imagine some venues we could play in if we get a tour? I mean, this place is just the tip of the iceberg."

Rami took in the buzzing excitement of the room, surrounded by his three best friends. The guys that had been with him on this journey from the very beginning, now dreaming of where they could take this little band, they started humbly so many years ago. These guys were his extended family, and he was lucky to have them in his life.

Speaking of luck, his good luck charm, Savanah, was nowhere to be seen in the crowd. When the clock struck midnight, Rami looked for her, but with the lights, he couldn't spot his beautiful girlfriend. He pulled out his phone and pulled up their text thread.

Rami: Hey babe, where are you? Didn't see you out there. I need my New Year's kiss.

He took a seat and waited for a while, looking at his phone, but no response. *Perhaps it's too loud for her to hear her phone.*

"Hey guys, I'm going to go out there and try to find Savanah." Rami informed them, striding over to the dressing room door.

Teasing Rex made kissing sounds and laughed gruffly. "Hey, if you see any hot girls by the stage door, tell them sexy Rexy is ready to party."

"Let me come with you." Layne suggested, giving Rex an annoyed look. Rex glanced at Steve, who shrugged him off.

Rami and Layne left the room, walking down the long corridor to the stage door. Exiting the backstage, a swarm of girls were standing by the door with a large intimidating security guard keeping an eye on them. When they opened the door to walk through, several girls pushed by them and the security guard noticing them waded through the rest of the girls disappearing behind the door to follow them backstage, presumably to kick them out of the venue. With no security around, Rami and Layne were instantly surrounded by girls shoving papers and pens in their faces, asking for autographs and holding up phones for selfies. Layne's eyes flitted to Rami with surprise as they signed their names on any items they were being handed and posed for pictures. For the most part, the fans were kind despite being demanding, and the press of more fans joining the swarm. Slowly, they were able to inch their way through without incident.

"Hey there Ramiro." a girl cooed, emphasizing each syllable of his name as she tightly gripped his arm, her hot breath far too close to his face for comfort.

"Hi! Did you enjoy the concert?" he asked, trying to appease her.

She leaned into him further, the smell of rum on her breath assaulting his senses. "I did, but it was missing something," she said, her hand splayed on his stomach. Rami furrowed his brows and turned to face her, breaking her hold, giving her a look to back away. The crowd pushed her closer to him again, and she flashed him a sultry smile, not bothered by his glare. "You never got a New Year's kiss," she slurred as she reached up with both hands, grabbed his face and planted a kiss on his lips, making him instantly recoil with shock and surprise. Yet he couldn't pull away, as her hands were already tangling in his hair and holding his head in place with surprising strength. Managing to peel his lips from hers, he glanced to the side, a shock of pretty pink hair catching his attention as his eyes focused to see Savanah and Dee standing there. Savanah's eyes were wide as saucers, a look of betrayal, incredulity, and disgust on her face. Her disbelief morphed quickly into overwhelming sadness as he watched tears form in her beautiful ocean blue eyes. The girl still had her hold on him and had now wrapped her arms around his waist. "Want to get out of here?" she asked loudly, running her hand over his chest.

Rami looked back to Savanah, her face painted with pure anguish, long tracks of tears now rolling down her face as she backed away from the crowd, away from him, turned and disappeared through the throngs of fans. Dee stood there for a beat, utter disappointment on her face as she shook her head, turned and followed her friend.

* * *

SAVANAH TURNED her phone to silent. *Another text from Rami.* It had been a month since their New Years Eve concert, and she didn't want to hear any of his lies. She was angry; she was hurt; she felt beyond betrayed by him. Every time she closed her eyes, all she saw was him holding that other woman, their lips locked in a passionate kiss. Then the woman's words would go on repeating in her head. *"Do you want to get out of here?"* Looping like circles through her consciousness. She loved Rami, and she had trusted him. She had given herself to him, mind, body, and soul. She had thought he had done the same for her, telling her he loved her, then claiming he was a virgin, too. *Was he? Or was it just a line to get her in bed? Was everything he said to me just a lie?*

Leaning her head back on the couch, she reached for a tissue, feeling the hot stinging tears prick her eyes again. She was so tired of crying; she just wanted this heart wrenching pain to go away. Dee, having seen the entire thing and after knowing where Savanah had run off to, had gone back and given Rami a piece of her mind. She appreciated her friend for that and although she had no idea exactly what their exchange was; she knew Dee was defending her honor. She was such a good friend. *Good friend. Friend.* Rami was her friend once. No more than a month ago she would have considered him one of her best friends. Her days revolved around him. When she was going to hear from or see him next. Looking back on their brief relationship, Savanah realized she was always waiting for him. Waiting for him to have time for her. Waiting for him to be there. She realized she was busy too, but she had spent all the time she once had for herself, just waiting for whatever sliver of time he could give her. Savanah felt duped. She had been bamboozled by his endearing lopsided smile, his handsome face, and all his flirtatious charms. He had ensnared her with his sweet and swoony dates and passionate kisses. Savanah let out a shaky sigh through the onslaught of tears. She knew what she needed to do. She wasn't going to be betrayed again. With a heart so heavy and broken, and hot bitter tears streaming down her face, she picked up her phone and replied to his last text.

"Rami, we need to talk. Let me know when you can meet me."

CHAPTER 10

ami pulled into the same diner they had gone to the night he and Savanah had consummated their relationship. The irony of this being the place she chose to meet now, not lost on him. It had been over a month since they last talked and when he got her text he had put everything aside to meet her and confront this. He was aware of how bad that night of the concert looked. He knew what she saw, but he also knew the truth and now that she agreed to see him, he was determined to make her see it, too. He would not let her go so easily.

Walking into the diner, Rami immediately spotted her. Her pretty pink hair was down and slung over one shoulder. She wore jeans, a white V-neck t-shirt and an oversized rose-pink cardigan. His spirits brightened at the sight of his girl, so beautiful as he approached her. Her eyes were downcast and rose slowly to meet his, red rimmed with excruciating sadness. Any hope he held onto squashed with one look into her anguished blue eyes. She didn't smile as he took a seat across from her. That beautiful smile he loved so much. That smile he loved to paint across her gorgeous face was absent and the realization of that made the pain he had caused clutch his heart and squeeze.

"Hi," he greeted softly, her gaze going down to her hands as she wrung them nervously. After spending every spare moment he had with Savanah over their five months together, he had observed her tells and could feel the anxiousness oozing off her. He could also see a slight tremble in her hands, and it took everything in him to not reach over and hold them, to comfort her. Without words, she reached beside her and lifted a shoebox onto the table, pushing it towards him. He looked at her unsure of how to respond, so he lifted the lid of the box to find his toothbrush, one of his leather cuffs, a notebook he left at her house and several cards and notes he had given her while they were together. He picked up one of the cards and opened it, reading the words in his head.

"You are my everything, Savanah. I love you."

An excruciating lump tightened in his throat as his eyes darted up to meet hers and he stared at her. "Are you breaking up with me?" he managed to croak out, his voice cracking with the question he couldn't believe he was asking as the burn of tears pierced his eyes, threatening to overflow.

She met his incredulous gaze, her eyes taking on a blank resolute stare, something he had never seen in them before. Her mouth settled into a grim line, and he could see a slight wobble of her chin, giving her away that she was finding her answer to his question hard to say. She cleared her throat to try to compose herself and replied, "I can't do this anymore, Rami. Yes, I'm breaking up with you."

Her words were like a stab to his heart. Like someone had stuck a knife so deep it stole his breath. Rami blinked slowly, the shock of her reply registering in his brain. He gulped down, not sure what to say. He wanted to fight. Fight for the woman he loved and the future he had envisioned for them. An overwhelming feeling of frustration consumed him as he asked. "You aren't even going to give me a chance to explain?"

"What's there to explain?" Savanah volleyed the question so quickly it made his head spin. She let out a shuddering sigh, her brows drawing together, as she replied. "I saw what I saw and there are always going to be girls fawning over you, Rami. Girls, more beautiful than me. The temptation will always be there."

"No one is more beautiful than you." Rami said, desperation edging his voice as he leaned forward to place his hand on her arm. "You're the only girl I see, Savanah. I love you."

Savanah flinched away from his touch, drew in a trembling breath, attempting to swallow back the tears. Her eyes rose to meet his, a bitter look chiding, as she wiped at a traitorous tear that rolled down her cheek and asked, "Then why are we here, right now, breaking up, Rami?"

Incredulity filled Rami's heart as he stared into the eyes of the only woman he ever loved. The only woman that ever mattered as the harsh reality of the moment slapped him square in the face. *She doesn't believe me. No matter what I say, she has made up her mind.*

Savanah cleared her throat, reached for her purse, rose

from the table and turned, staring down at him one last time with pure anguish in her blue depths as she whispered simply, "Goodbye Rami." Then she turned from him, walked out of the diner and out of his life, leaving him shattered. All dreams of a future with Savanah, a pile of broken shards on the floor.

* * *

"DUDE, THESE NEW SONGS ARE DARK." Steve commented, paging through the lyrics in Rami's notebook. "Ever since you and Savanah broke up you've been writing some very broody shit."

Rami squinted at his bandmates and gave them a shrug, feigning off Steve's comment as he asked, "Do you guys have a problem with that?"

"I don't. I personally love the dark shit you're writing. Maybe breaking up with your pink bunny was a good thing?" Rex stated with a smirk.

"Don't call her that." Rami growled at him, his whole "mad at the world" demeanor not his usual MO.

"Have you seen or talked to her at all?" Layne asked, frowning at his friend. "Did you try to explain to her what happened?"

"Of course I did," Rami replied, giving Layne a glare. "She had already made up her mind that we were done so she wouldn't listen."

"I'm just saying I was there and saw how that girl attacked you. You couldn't get away if you tried. She was relentless and had a vice grip on you." Layne added, picking up his guitar.

Rami gave him a look, imploring him to stop talking about it, his eyes fiery with a combination of frustration and sadness. Layne continued, oblivious to the mounting tension surrounding him, "But I could see how she could misunderstand. I mean, from her point of view it must have looked pretty bad."

With his words, Rami snatched his notebook from Steve and grabbed his guitar, stomping out of the garage and over to his car, slamming the door as he got inside.

"Fuck, Layne." Rex chided with a scowl, hitting the cymbals on his drum set as they watched Rami peel out of the driveway, tires squealing, kicking up dust and gravel as he went.

* * *

SAVANAH LIFTED her head from her work dressing a window display to see three of her best customers coming into the boutique. Bea, Ever and Whitney came through the door, the sound of their happy chatter and laughter warming Savanah's heart.

"Hello, ladies! I haven't seen you all in so long!" Savanah exclaimed, giving each of them a hug in greeting. "What brings you in here today?"

"The wedding is just four months away, and we want to know what kind of ideas you have for the bridesmaid dresses." Bea asked eagerly, clapping her hands together.

"I've got so many ideas!" Savanah exclaimed excitedly. "I put a few samples in the back if you want to check them out. Just let me slip back there and get them." Savanah returned a few minutes later with a rolling rack of dresses, all in various shades and prints of pink.

"Wow, these are all so amazing!" Ever exclaimed, taking in a sleek silky dress with a tea rose print.

"Can we try some on?" Whitney asked, lifting one option off the rack and admiring it.

"Absolutely! Go right ahead." Savanah replied, gesturing to her change rooms at the back of the shop as Ever and Whitney grabbed a couple of dresses each and went to try them on.

Bea lingered next to her, and she could see Bea surveying her in her peripheral. Savanah turned to her, feigning a smile.

"Are you doing okay?" she asked softly, empathy in her eyes. "You haven't come by in a while."

Savanah glanced down at her hands, wringing them anxiously, frustrated that Bea could read her so easily. "I'm okay," she answered simply. The truth was, she was the farthest thing from okay. Her heart was shattered, and she fought every day with both animosity towards and her longing for Rami. It was a confusing state to be in.

"You know you can talk to me if you need to." Bea offered, placing a comforting hand on her arm. "It wasn't so long ago that I was in a dark place too, after I thought your brother and I were over. I know if it wasn't for Ever and Whitney, I'm not sure I would've gotten through it all."

Savanah turned to Bea, revealing her forlorn sadness, and replied, "The difference is that Garrett was all in on you. He was committed fully to you. I don't know if Rami was ever fully committed to me."

"What makes you say that? I mean, from my interaction with him, from what he told Garrett and from what Marnie has said, he was already thinking big picture with you." Bea shared, her eyes never leaving Savanah's.

"When was Rami talking to Garrett?" Savanah asked, her brows drawing together with confusion.

"He and Garrett would get together for lunch when you two started dating. I think he was asking for advice on your dates. That was my understanding. I know he wanted his insight, as he was determined to make them special and memorable." Bea answered. "If you ask me, any guy that is going to go to all that trouble to plan dates reenacting your favorite romantic movies must be thinking more long term. Why would he go to all that effort only to date you for a short time?"

Savanah thought about that for a moment. Those epic romantic dates seemed like a lifetime ago already. She thought about how much effort he put in and knew Bea was right, but that didn't change the fact that everything had now changed between them. Rami lived in a world that made her uncomfortable and reminded her of the life she walked away from.

Savanah wiped at a traitorous tear that escaped through her lashes and met Bea's gaze as she replied, an aching cry edging her voice. "And yet, somehow here I am with broken trust and a broken heart."

Bea's brilliant green eyes mirrored her sadness as she curled herself around Savanah in a hug, telling her she would get through this. Savanah swallowed down the lump forming in her throat, tamping down the building emotions, determined not to cry another tear over Rami Perez.

* * *

EVERYTHING YOU KNEAD was insanely busy all day and Rami was thankful for the distraction. He loved working here and although he wasn't picking up as many shifts as he did in the beginning, he wasn't ready to give up his job here just yet. This job grounded him. Made him feel normal and not like the lead singer of a band on the cusp of stardom. Plus, Marnie still needed his help, and he would do anything for his sister.

He flipped over the sign saying they were closed, then he locked the door and turned to clean up before he left for the night.

"Rami, if you have a few minutes, come back here and chat with me," Marnie called from the back kitchen.

He opened the swinging door of the commercial kitchen to find his sister perched on a stool, piping bag in hand, her eyes zoned in on decorating a wedding cake. She looked up from her work and gestured for him to grab a stool and take a seat. He complied, and she set down her piping bag to give him her full attention.

"What happened between you and Savanah?" Marnie asked bluntly as she held up her hand and shook her head. "I know, I know, you two broke up months ago, but you've only been giving me the short answers. I want to hear the whole story."

Rami put his head in his hands, his fingers sliding through his curls. "I fucked up," he said raggedly, his voice cracking. "I fucked up bad, Marnie. The band started getting more popular, and I put all my efforts towards the band and forgot about putting effort towards her. Then New Years happened, and it sealed the deal. She broke it off."

Marnie moved her stool around her workspace to sit next to her brother, rubbing her hand over his back supportively as he hung his head low. "What happened on New Years?"

He looked up at Marnie, his brown eyes red rimmed and a tear rolled down his face. "There was this girl..." he began.

Before he could continue, Marnie smacked him on the back of the head. "Estupido!" she shouted. "Did you cheat on Savanah?"

"Fuck no!" Rami exclaimed, getting up from the stool, rubbing the back of his head and distancing himself from Marnie's punishing hand. "After the show, I left backstage to find Savanah, and the backstage was filled with fans. Layne was with me, and we obliged them by signing autographs and taking selfies. Some drunk girl came up to me and put a vice grip on my arm, which I thought was innocent at first. It's not like girls haven't made passes at me at shows before, but this girl was persistent. She got up in my face and before I knew it, she was kissing me. I swear I never kissed her back, but she grabbed ahold of my head, gripping my hair so tight, so it may have looked like I was. I don't know. She basically pounced on me and that's when Savanah appeared. She saw her kiss me, thought I was kissing her back, and when the girl propositioned me further, Savanah turned and ran off. She just assumed I was unfaithful or going to be. I don't know. She wouldn't hear my side of the story.

"Yikes, Rami, that is bad. This girl that jumped on you, you had no idea who she was?" Marnie asked for clarification.

"No idea. She was completely drunk and the security that was guarding the stage door was distracted by some girls that snuck into the back, so no one was there to get her off me. Layne would have helped but when he turned this girl had me in a lip lock, so he pretty much saw what Savanah saw," Rami added, taking his seat again next to Marnie. "The only difference was he knew how intense the entire situation was and understood what happened. Savanah didn't and now she thinks I was cheating or was about to cheat on her. Fuck Marnie, I would never betray her like that. Never."

Marnie shook her head, and furrowed her brow, as she looked into the eyes of her brother and replied, "Honestly, Rami, now that I know the total story, I would've had a hard time with what happened too. You must put yourself in Savanah's shoes. She is completely in love with you, and she comes around the corner to find another woman has her hands and lips all over you. She also has been thrown into all the hoopla and craziness that comes with what you do. I've had conversations with Savanah about what the scene was like when she was modeling, and it was a lot. Underage girls being taken advantage of, crazy parties, drugs, not to mention all the criticism, attacking her body image constantly. Then there was the competition between girls. Super catty mean girl stuff. With you being thrown into the public eye and having the beginning of your love story out there for anyone to watch, it puts a spotlight back on her and sadly has opened her up to very public scrutiny again."

Rami looked at his sister, his eyes wide as he replied, "She had never really explained all that went down during her years of modeling, just that the lifestyle was not for her. And she never told me how much our fandom was affecting her."

"Did you ever ask her, though?" Marnie questioned as she gave him a chiding look. "If you would have, I know she would have been forthcoming with you. Savanah has a sweet, quiet, and calm demeanor, and I know she deals with anxiety and insecurities stemming from her past career. She and I talked about it, and I asked her about her past. From what she told me, it was a lot for a young woman barely of age to deal with. She was thrown into this lifestyle that made her very uncomfortable. A lifestyle that, if you look at it, is comparable to the lifestyle you are being thrown into. As your sister, I know you and trust that you have a good head on your shoulders and will take all the fame coming your way in stride. I know your convictions and how we were raised. Because of that, I'm not concerned about you sleeping around with groupies or abusing drugs or alcohol, as I know that's not you. Savanah on the other hand, doesn't have that kind of history with you. You two had known each other as children, barely reconnected as adults, and hadn't had the chance to build a solid foundation of trust."

"Then when our views started to grow, and our videos went viral, I started spending weeks with my band and only giving her the little time I had left," he said, giving his head a shake. "I'm an idiot."

"Yeah, you are," Marnie agreed with a sardonic smile, putting her hand on his back in reassurance. "But you can try to make it right. Why don't you start by reaching out to her as a friend? You two started as friends, and it doesn't mean you can't be friends again. Start there and take things slow, then see where things go. Build a bond of trust with each other again."

Rami took in his sister's words and thought about how in such a short time they went from being reunited, to dating, to I love you, into an intimate relationship and then he dropped her. Literally dropped her like she wasn't important and didn't matter to him. Like she wasn't worth giving his time to. Marnie was right. He needed to start back from square one and this time build a better foundation with her. *Now to just get Savanah to talk to me.*

CHAPTER 11

The late spring weather was unseasonably hot for the end of May and Savanah was cursing herself for not changing out of her work clothes to make this delivery. The humidity was hot and sticky, and she was already sweating buckets before she even reached her destination. She turned down the road leading to Layne's house just outside of Primrose and felt her nerves build, causing her pulse to thrum in her ears. She took a deep calming breath to try to steady her growing anxiety as she gave herself an internal pep talk. *This is just a quick and easy drop off, that's it. Just a few words to confirm that they're still playing Garrett and Bea's wedding, drop off the deposit cheque and I'm out of there. No need to have an in-depth conversation. No need to linger around the band. Just get done what I promised Garrett I would do. Just doing my job as their wedding planner. That's it.*

Reaching Layne's driveway, Savanah immediately heard the band in mid-song, the strong beat of the drum, the smooth sound of the keyboard and the guitars cutting through the country quiet. Rami's voice carried on the breeze, and she stopped at the end of the driveway with her foot on the brake as she closed her eyes a moment and took in his smooth, sultry voice. A voice she loved and could listen to all day. *You're not doing this Savanah;* she chided as she took in another quick calming breath and released the brake before turning onto Layne's driveway.

She could see their cars, including Rami's RX-7 parked in a cluster and between the cars, she could see the garage door was open. She had been here once before and knew the detached garage was their makeshift studio for practicing. She parked and craned her neck to glance in her rearview mirror, tucking the loose strands of hair that escaped her ponytail behind her ears. Determined to get this over and done with, she exited her vehicle with the envelope her brother gave her in hand. Striding up to the open garage, the entire band came into view. Layne, noticing her first and nudging Rami in the side as he sang. When he noticed her, he stopped mid song, his face dropping as she approached. His bandmates stopped playing and a thick silence fell on the group. Savanah swallowed down her nervousness, her eyes darting from band member to band member acknowledging each of them despite the awkwardness, then settling on Rami before she spoke, her tone businesslike and aloof.

"Sorry to interrupt, but Garrett asked me to drop this off. It's the deposit for Garrett and Bea's wedding. I'm assuming you're still planning on playing?" she asked, holding the envelope up for the entire band to see.

Layne, Rex, and Steve, eyes darting between her and Rami and all three answered with a collaborative yes.

Savanah boldly turned her gaze to Rami and looked him dead in the eyes, trying desperately not to show him the pain that still constricted her heart. "Will you still be singing?" she asked, her question coming out on a shuddering breath as her heart jack hammered in her chest.

Rami softened his gaze, his eyes transitioning from shock at seeing her to his signature sweetness. *I fell for that sweetness once, not again.* Savanah gritted her teeth. "Well?" she asked, raising her chin to him, her eyes flashing with determined frustration.

"Of course, anything for Garrett and Bea." Rami answered, his voice coming out gravelly as he slowly approached her. She held out the envelope between them and he took it from her, looking up and meeting her eyes. Beautiful brown eyes that could melt her more than the sweltering heat of the burgeoning summer. She hadn't seen those eyes in five months, the same amount of time it took for them to date and fall in love. The irony of that was not lost on her.

Not losing her composure, she glanced amongst his bandmates and added, "I'll email you the details." Turning on her heel, she walked away, letting out a shaky exhale when she was almost back to her car.

"Wait." Rami's voice sounded behind her. Stopping in her tracks, she closed her eyes praying he wasn't right behind her. "Wait," he whispered, his deep voice close and like a song to her heart. Hot tears welled up, and she sucked in a shuddering breath, in a desperate attempt to steady her emotions she swallowed down hard. *I can't let him see me cry.* She turned around to face him, knowing her glossy eyes would give all her emotions away. Seeing the tears in her eyes, Rami took a step back, reading that she needed some distance and met her anguished gaze, his eyes also glistening with unshed tears, as he stuttered. "I… I just wanted to say, I'm so sorry. I'm not going to stand here trying to explain what happened, but I just want you to know how sorry I am and that I hope we can one day be friends again. Because above all else, Savanah, I miss my friend."

Her eyes searched his, her head waging all-out war with her heart. She wasn't going to try to lie to herself right now. She missed his friendship, too. Out of every-thing, all that they had experienced together, losing their friendship left the largest hole in her heart. Despite this, she needed to process and sort out her feelings before she decided whether or not his friendship was something she would bring back into her life. "I'll think about it," she whispered, her voice breaking with each word.

Rami nodded and stuffed his hands in his pockets as he looked down at his boots. He lingered there a few beats, as if wanting to say more, but not having the words. Finally, he turned, striding back to the garage, glancing back once to see her go.

* * *

Email to Savanah Smithfield @ Pretty Things Boutique from Layne Stark:

Hey Savanah,

Thank you for dropping off the deposit yesterday for Bea and Garrett's wedding. On behalf of myself and the band, we're looking forward to being part of their special day.

This email is completely out of character for me as I don't usually meddle in the lives of my friends, but seeing your interaction with Rami when you came by the garage yesterday it was hard to watch. Rami is like a brother to me, and seeing him hurting and missing you so much has been painful. I feel compelled to write this to you as I think this email may help you understand Rami more and understand what happened at the New Year's concert. So here goes, this is everything that happened that night.

Before you saw Rami with that girl, you need to know we were completely overwhelmed by the fans waiting for us at the stage door. The security wasn't there to help control the crowd, and we were left to try to make our way through it the only way we knew how, which was by fulfilling their requests for selfies and autographs. We had never had that level of fanfare before, and neither one of us was prepared for the onslaught. The girl that you saw kiss Rami literally pounced on him. He was taken completely off guard, and never once did he give her any reason to think that he wanted her to do that. He was completely ambushed, and you simply walked up at the wrong time. I know how bad it probably looked to you and I understand you being upset. Truly I do. I just think you should have heard Rami out. I have known Rami since we were kids, and we started this band together. Rami is someone who has convictions and stands by them. He has integrity and is not easily influenced by others. He has his own mind and stands strong in his beliefs. He cares deeply for his family and friends, and he has never been in love until you. I have never seen my friend happier than when you came into his life. And I have never seen him in more pain than when you walked out of his life. He misses you, Savanah, and maybe I'm completely overstepping here, but I think you miss him, too. Give him a chance, hear him out, and please don't write him off. You both deserve to be happy.

Layne

* * *

JULY HAD ARRIVED, and Garrett and Bea's wedding was only two weeks away. Bea was working, so Garrett and Amelia invited Savanah out for breakfast at the Eazy Café in Primrose. Savanah had never been to "The Eazy " as the locals called it and she had to admit the decades-old Café with its small-town retro diner look, had its charms.

"I can't believe it's only two weeks until you're married!" Savanah exclaimed before popping a hash brown into her mouth.

"I am so excited!" Amelia said cutely, beaming from her seat next to her dad.

Savanah smiled at her niece, already sticky from her syrupy pancakes.

"It has come on so fast and yet somehow not fast enough. I can't wait to marry Bea." Garrett declared, his eyes sparkling and smile wide. "And you have been amazing at helping us plan this wedding. I mean, I think neither of us knew where to begin and you just took over. I have no doubt it will be incredible."

"It's been fun and honestly, I've loved figuring out the details and customizing it to you both," she mused, meeting her brother's eyes. "Maybe Pretty Things needs to expand to include party planning. I've been giving it a lot of thought lately and maybe I don't need a storefront anymore. My curating services have already surpassed what we do as a storefront this year. Perhaps I need to rethink my business plan."

"Well, you're good at it. Not just with fashion, but with party planning. You have thought out every single detail with our wedding and your organization is next level." Garrett complimented. "Are you thinking maybe an online business, where you keep a home office and go to your customers or have them come to you? You could still curate fashion but offer party planning as your main service. It doesn't have to be just weddings, either. Birthdays, anniversaries, corporate events perhaps. Honestly, the sky's the limit."

"That's where my passion lies at the moment." she said, tapping her chin in thought for a moment before offering her brother a knowing smile. "I honestly think it would do really well."

"I think that's an amazing idea. You have a mind for business, and you're so good at what you do. Perhaps without the storefront, it would give you more time to focus on other things too," he said, his brows raised as he brought his coffee cup to his lips.

"What kinds of "other" things?" Savanah asked, squinting her eyes and making air quotes with her fingers.

"Perhaps if you didn't work so much and isolate yourself the rest of the time, you would have time for a relationship. Perhaps rekindle things with Rami." Garrett suggested, a look of concern in his eyes. "I know you're going to be annoyed by me saying this, but I don't think you're over him, and I know 100% that he's not over you. He really misses you."

"Rami is the best!" Amelia exclaimed, her smile wide.

Savanah glanced affectionately at Amelia and back to her brother, opened her mouth to protest, and she closed her mouth again. *When did my family become 'Team Rami'?*

Garrett held up his hand to her. "I know, I know, I have no idea what exactly happened, but maybe you two could start with friendship and go from there. Besides, I think any guy that literally watches your favorite movie a dozen times so he can memorize the lines to your favorite scene may deserve a second chance."

"You were the one that told him about that movie, weren't you?" Savanah questioned.

"Guilty as charged. Who else would know about IKEA? Dani was the one that introduced you to that movie," he added with a wistful smile.

Garrett mentioning his late wife was rare these days. The memory of her and Dani curling up under a blanket with a big bowl of popcorn came back to her, and she smiled. "I had forgotten about that. I miss Dani." she said sadly of her late sister-in-law they tragically lost because of a drunk driver.

Garrett offered her a melancholy smile and looked down at Amelia with affection, memories obviously coming back to him as he answered, "Me too."

Savanah thought about Garrett and Dani and how precious life was. Rami was, at one point, very important to her, and she was starting to see a future with him. *Was I too quick to assume he was guilty of something he wasn't? Did I let my judgements and past experiences cloud my decision?* Savanah had so many confusing thoughts and questions running through her head all at once. One thing she knew is that she loved Rami once and if she was being honest with herself, she still had feelings for him. First as a friend, then more, and that he was too important to her to completely erase from her life.

* * *

THE WEDDING DAY was finally here, and Primrose was buzzing with excitement. Savanah walked into the church sanctuary, truly proud of what she had put together for her brother and soon to be sister-in-law. The sanctuary screamed *Pretty in Pink,* and she had no doubt that Bea was going to love it.

Savanah checked her watch. The bridal party was set to arrive anytime, and guests would likely start arriving in about 30 minutes. She wanted this time to just admire her hard work. A quiet time to enjoy the calm before the storm. She walked down the aisle, taking in the delicate pink and cream roses, yards of draped tulle and the gorgeous backdrop where Garrett and Bea would soon say their vows in front of a spectacular cascade of roses in every shade of pink. She made her way over to the piano, the sheet music for two 80s classics from Phil Collins and Hall & Oates already there. She smiled and put her hands on the keys, pressing one with her index finger.

"Are you going to play something?" a deep voice asked, making her look up in surprise. Rami stood there, his brown eyes twinkling and his handsome lopsided smile curving his lips. He was dressed nicely in a blue button-down shirt and black dress pants. She glanced down at his combat boots and smiled with amusement as she pressed another key on the piano. He sauntered over to her, gesturing for her to slide over on the piano bench. She obliged as he took a seat next to her. She could feel the heat radiate off him and her pulse quickened as the scent of Sandalwood enveloped her senses. He put his hands on the keys and started to play a tune unfamiliar to her.

"That's beautiful." She murmured gently.

He stopped playing and turned his head to meet her eyes. She locked onto them as he answered. "Just something I'm working on right now."

"I like it."

Rami's smile turned melancholy, and he turned his attention back to the keys for a moment. The unsaid words between them, thick. He looked up again, meeting her gaze with pain and regret in their depths as a confession tumbled from his lips, raw and strangled. "I miss having you in my life."

His words gripped her heart and squeezed painfully. Savanah looked down at his hands still on the keys and she reached over, placing her hand on his. "I've missed you too," she whispered, mirroring his sadness. "I would like to be friends again."

His eyes brightened, the sadness morphing into something hopeful yet cautious as he replied with a half-smile. "I would like that."

Hearing the doors to the church open and the sound of familiar chatter echo from the front entrance, Savanah slid off the bench and turned to him, "Can we talk later? The bridal party just arrived."

"Yes." he replied, sliding to the middle of the bench and picking up the sheet music for the wedding. "We can catch up later. I've got a job to do." he winked as he played the prelude music in preparation for the wedding guests to arrive.

* * *

With what could only be described as an epic wedding and everyone's hearts and bellies full of heartwarming speeches and delicious food, it was now time for the party to begin. The sun was setting, with bands of pink, purple and orange twisting in the sky, the view from the Prairie Sky Acres front lawn beyond beautiful. Rami took in the stunning sunset as he slipped his guitar over his body and looked at his bandmates, who were already in place. Tonight, felt full of promise, like a tide was turning and he felt hopeful for the first time in the past six months since his breakup with Savanah. Rami was ready for a new chapter and now he was ready to entertain the guests, many of which he knew from this wonderful Primrose community he was so proud to be a part of. As he turned and stepped up to the mic, he smiled as he surveyed the familiar faces, his eyes landing on Savanah's big beautiful blue eyes.

She smiled at him with kindness, forgiveness and warmth and he thought his heart may burst from his chest as he stepped to the microphone and said, "Garrett and Bea, we're excited to be here to perform for you and all your amazing guests! We're Prairie Sound, and we're going to start with a Bon Jovi classic. I'm sure you're going to recognize." He turned to the band, nodded, and returned to the mic, shouting "2,3,4!" He sang as the entire band joined him with the beginning of "Born to be my Baby" a crowd pleaser and a special request from the bride. The guests crowded the dance floor as the party erupted. Savanah was dancing with Marnie, Ever and Whitney. Savanah glanced up at him and meet his eyes as he belted out, "You were born to be my baby, and baby, I was made to be your man!" Her eyes sparkled in the dimming light of day and the guilt, pain and hurt he carried on his shoulders from the past six months eased with knowing she was going to let him back in. Back into her life and hopefully someday back into her heart.

SAVANAH SAT AT AN EMPTY TABLE, taking in the full dance floor, the chatter, the laughter, the wide smiles. Everyone was having fun, the atmosphere was joyful and festive. She caught the eye of Bea on the dance floor, and she winked as she mouthed 'thank you' to her. Pride filled her chest as she surveyed what she had accomplished with this event. With its success, the way forward leading her down a different path in her career became clear. Tonight, she had been approached by three couples, two for weddings and one for a 50th anniversary, all wanting her help with their events. Perhaps she had found her calling.

"Hey, there you are." Rami's rich voice sounded beside her as he took a seat next to her, two colas in his hands.

He handed one to her, and she met his gaze. "Thank you."

"No problem," he replied, looking at the dance floor like she had been moments earlier. "You planned an incredible wedding."

"Thanks." she replied with a smile as she leaned against the backrest of the chair, taking a sip from the straw of her cola before she added. "I've decided to close down my boutique as of September 1st."

He turned his entire body towards her, his eyes full of questions. "Why? Your boutique is your life. You love that place."

"I do, but I want to have a life beyond it. I'm still going to be doing my thing, curating fashion, but I'm going to start an event planning business. I won't need a storefront for that, as I can do everything online and meet directly with clients. Bring myself to them."

Rami sat back in his seat as he responded. "Wow, that's a great idea."

She nodded and took another sip of her drink. "I think it will help me find more balance between work and personal life."

Rami nodded his head and glanced her way, meeting her gaze, "That's part of what broke us, wasn't it? Me not knowing how to balance the band and being with you."

She met his gaze, knowing now was the time to be completely candid, if not brutally honest. "That was part of it. Truthfully, I always felt like an afterthought."

Rami winced, ran his hand through his thick curls and let out a long breath as he shook his head. "I messed up the best thing that ever happened to me," he said, looking down at his hands with furrowed brows.

A stillness fell on them as they gazed out onto the guests, having fun on the dance floor, and simply sat together for a long time in contemplative silence before Rami spoke. "I'm not sure I can promise perfect balance to anyone, as I've so much to figure out myself, but I know what I did wrong with us and if given the chance, I would like the opportunity to fix this." he pointed from himself to her. "I don't know if you'll let me into your heart ever again, but I would like to see you again, even just as friends. I miss spending time with you."

"I think we should try friendship for now," she agreed, reaching out for his hand and threading her fingers with his.

He smiled at her and leaned in, placing an affectionate kiss on the cheek. The feel of his soft lips against her skin making her head spin. His hot breath at her ear as he said, "I know we're no longer a couple, but please ask me to play your song. I really want to sing it for you."

Savanah's breath caught; the memory of the promise made to her so long ago was a sweet one. She breathed out her question. "Can you sing me my song?"

Rami pushed his chair back and smiled as he got to his feet, flashing her a playful wink. "Good, because I added it to our playlist!"

Savanah giggled as he waved down his bandmates and they made their way to the stage for their second set.

They all took their places, and Rami grabbed the mic. "Is everyone having fun tonight?" The guests cheered in response. "We're going to start this next set with a special request from the remarkable woman who planned every detail of this outstanding wedding. She is the sister of the groom, the wedding planner extraordinaire and one of the best people I know, Savanah Smithfield." The guests clapped and cheered, all eyes turning to her. "As we continue this celebration under a prairie sky full of stars, this one's for you, Savanah. Your favorite song!"

Steve started on the keyboard playing the familiar intro of the song and everyone smiled, turned to Savanah seated at the back of the tent, her cheeks taking on a rosy hue from the attention.

Marnie appeared beside her and put her hand out to her. "Come join us on the dance floor. You have to dance to your song."

Savanah smiled at her friend and took her hand as she led her to the dance floor. All the familiar faces she knew from Primrose there, Ben, Ever, Hayden, Whitney, Marnie, Bea's brother Davis, Bea, Garrett and even Amelia. Everyone danced their hearts out as they sang along with Prairie Sound. Savanah closed her eyes, feeling the music, Rami's smooth rich voice belting out the words she adored as the tempo picked up and everyone cheered. Savanah danced like she had never danced before, light, carefree, the weight on her chest finally lifting and hope in her heart.

CHAPTER 12

With Pretty Things officially closing their doors on September 1st, the entire month of August was dedicated to winding down the business. With her lease agreement for the space coming up for renewal in September, the timing to close the doors of her boutique turned out to be perfect.

During this time, Dee was offered a term teaching position at St. Augustine Regional High School, starting with the new school year and any other staff she had were casual. The part that was the hardest was the sadness of her loyal customers that loved to come in to visit and comb the racks for treasures. She was going to miss them, but she knew many of the relationships she had cultivated over the few years she owned her boutique would follow her to her online business. In fact, when asked what she would be doing now, many were excited about her new business model and promised they would contact her for the perfect outfit for their next event.

Savanah walked around her now empty shop. Most

items had been sold and anything else had been boxed up and moved out already. She grabbed the large store sign and tucked it under her arm as she made her way to the door, taking one last look at her beloved boutique as she exited and locked the door for the last time. As she turned around, she was surprised to see Rami standing just down the sidewalk from her shop, a large takeout bag in his hand. He held it up, Ling Family Chinese Restaurant on the front of the bag and said, "I thought you could use some food therapy."

Savanah strode over to him, a look of gratitude on her face. "Thank you, Rami. It's been a heavy day. I'm so exhausted and hungry." She said as her stomach took that moment to let out a little growl.

Rami laughed and replied. "I got here in the nick of time, then. How about we enjoy this in the park? It's a nice night and I have a blanket in the car that we can sit on."

"Sounds great." She agreed as she held up the sign she was holding. "Maybe I can unload this into my car, and we can walk to the park. It's only a few blocks away."

He nodded and followed her, his car parked behind hers on the street. As she put the sign into her trunk, he pulled the blanket out of the back of his car and handed it to her. They walked quietly for the first blocks, neither quite sure what to say. Savanah let out an audible sigh and Rami turned to her; his eyes full of compassion as he said. "Today must've been a hard day."

She nodded and replied, "The hardest, but also bittersweet. I guess because I know I'm moving on to something amazing."

"You're really doing it then, the event planning?" he asked, his concern morphing into a smile.

"Yep, I booked two events from Garrett and Bea's wedding already. I have a wedding next summer, a 50th anniversary in November, and I have a huge list of customers who want me to help them find outfits for their upcoming events in the next few months." She replied. "It's not a lot, but it's a start."

"I may have another event for you to plan if you're down to do it. It's not fancy like a wedding or anything, but our first album is finally being released at the beginning of October and the band and I were wondering if you could plan us an album drop party." He asked with a hopeful tone. "It could be a big event, lots of local contacts, and it would be a great way to launch your new business. Sylvio offered to have it at the Pickled Pig. Of course, you would be paid for your services."

She stopped walking and turned to him, a smile on her face as she answered, "I would love to plan your party."

They continued down the sidewalk, reaching their destination. Turning into the park, the same park where they reunited just over a year ago. They found a nice place to set up the blanket and Savanah spread it out before she took a seat criss crossing her legs in front of her. Rami sat down next to her and opened the takeout bag, handing her a LaCroix and pulling out one for himself. Removing the food from the takeout bag, the smell of deep-fried spring rolls, teriyaki noodles, shrimp fried rice, spicy Szechuan chicken and beef and broccoli all wafted from the containers. Savanah breathed in deeply.

"You got all my favorites." She said, peeking into each container and licking her lips. "This all feels very déjà vu."

"I remembered," he said with a smile, holding up a fork and some chopsticks.

She grabbed the chopsticks with a giggle and ripped open the package. After breaking the chopsticks apart, as she picked up the beef and broccoli container and stabbed a piece of broccoli bringing it to her mouth. Her eyes rolled back, and she sighed happily, shaking her shoulders in approval as she chewed.

Rami laughed as he grabbed a spring roll with his fingers. "No plates, I like it!"

They ate together, passing the containers between them, their conversation light as the sun set behind them and the faint glimmer of stars dappled the sky. There were lots of people on the walking paths and lounging in the park, the early September breeze making it a pleasant night to be outside. Rami packed up the leftover food and tucked it away in the takeout bag, glancing at Savanah, whose eyes were raised to the heavens. The stars now twinkling bright against the burgeoning night sky. He set the takeout bag aside and leaned back on his elbows, stretching his long legs out in front of him, crossing them at the ankles. She leaned back on her palms, inclining her back to get a better view of the beauty before them.

"You know, whenever I see a sky like this and feel that chilled breeze that you get at the end of summer, I always think of all those years we would meet on the dock at Camp Clearwater." he mused.

Savanah smiled wistfully at the memory and let out a giggle. "I'm shocked we never got caught."

"Never in five years." he added, mirroring her laughter. "Remember how exhausted we would both be the next day when our parents would come and pick us up?"

"I would always fall asleep in the car on the way home," she added.

"Me too." he laughed, his voice turning wistful. "I wouldn't have traded those nights for anything, though."

"They were the best." She whispered, laying her head down completely on the blanket, the expansive night sky speckled with stars enrobing her in their quiet comfort. Rami lay down next to her, his hand reaching for hers. Their fingers threaded as they lay there, two friends reminiscing, their joint memories consoling them.

PRAIRIE SOUND WALKED into the Pickled Pig and their jaws slacked.

"Holy shit!" Steve exclaimed, his bandmates all echoing the sentiment.

The beloved honky tonk bar they frequented was transformed into a sleek and swanky nightclub. The expansive room had a large stage set up for them to perform with a background of their new album cover. There were high tables for people to stand and mingle and a social media area to take pictures with life size cut outs of each member of Prairie Sound. A kiosk was set up for merchandise to be purchased along with their new album and an area set up with long tables for food.

"Your girl sure outdid herself." Sylvio commented as

he acknowledged the band from behind the bar. "We even have a custom drink for each of you. Check it out."

Layne picked up the laminated menu that appeared to be on every table.

Ramiro – Michelada – Lime Juice, Mexican Beer, Chili Powder, and hot sauce

Layne – Old Fashioned – Canadian Whiskey, Bitters, Simple Syrup

Steve – Prosecco Negroni – Vermouth, Campari and Champagne

Rex – Canadian Beer – Ice cold Labatt Blue

"This is fuckin' awesome!" Rex commented, glancing over Layne's shoulder. "But who is the Pink Lady for?"

The last drink on the menu was listed as:

Pink Lady – Vodka, Raspberry juice and coconut rum

Sylvio laughed and pointed to the corner of the menu, then replied, "Pink Lady Productions, Savanah's new event planning company."

Rami swiped the menu, which Rex was now holding, and looked at her new logo, whispering, "She did it."

"That girl of yours is incredible. A real one in a million. She has literally thought of every detail for this party." Sylvio added, his eyes meeting Rami. "You better hold tight to that one."

Sylvio's words gut punched him, his chest tightening painfully. Whether or not he and Savanah were together as a couple, Savanah was his girl, no question. Layne glanced at him, noticing his shift in mood, and put a supportive hand on his shoulder. Rami looked up at his long-time friend and smiled in appreciation, knowing Layne understood how he was feeling.

A catcall whistle sounded from behind the bar as Sylvio turned to the door, his eyes wide as he declared, "The Pink Lady has arrived."

The entire band turned to the door to see Savanah dressed in a hot pink leather bustier catsuit with a matching cropped leather fringed jacket and sexy pink high heels. Her pink hair was fashioned in a sleek high ponytail and her makeup was sultry and sexy, enhancing her flawless skin and mesmerizing ocean blue eyes. Her pillowy lips were the same gorgeous pink color as her catsuit and Rami's mouth grew dry as he took her in.

She surveyed the room, a grin curving her kissable lips as she noticed the band by the bar. She zoned in on them and sashayed her way over, her eyes dancing playfully with each step and swish of her ponytail. As she approached, Rami had to remind himself to breathe, his eyes not leaving the complete bombshell coming their way.

"Hot damn, pink bunny. Someone needs to call the fire department." Rex announced, looking her up and down with approval as he made a sizzling sound between his teeth.

Savanah cocked a brow at Rex and let a giggle escape. "From you, Rex, I'll take that as a compliment. What do you think?" she asked, turning, her eyes roaming over the bar with a look of pride on her face. "Not too bad for the first ever event by Pink Lady Productions."

"It's incredible, Savanah! Seriously awesome." Steve answered, all the guys nodding, Rami still quiet and trying to get his bearings.

"Just to fill you guys in on what's happening tonight.

The Blue Corn will be here in a few minutes with the food. Marnie has outdone herself with desserts and should be arriving anytime." Savanah informed her tone of voice all business. "Rami's parents have volunteered to run the food area. Garrett and Bea are running the merchandise booth and Dee is running the social media nook. We have created a hashtag for this event – #prairiesoundrocks. The front door security has the guest list. We have around 250 people RSVP'd to this event, including your agent, a handful of Manitoba DJs, reporters from all the local newspapers, tv and radio stations. As well, we have some local industry producers that will be attending which your agent has invited. All your families are coming, and the rest of the invited guests are friends and radio station contest winners." She let out a long exhale and feigned wiping sweat from her brow. "And I think that's it."

The band stood in front of her, their eyes wide and mouths agape, Rami finally finding his voice was the first to speak. "Savanah, you've outdone yourself."

She met his gaze as she replied, "My pleasure." The door to the bar opened and Rami's family walked in carrying large trays of food followed by Marnie with the desserts and Savanah walked off to meet them. Rami could not look away as he followed the sexy sway of her hips and the long expanse of her leather clad legs as she went.

THE ALBUM DROP party was in full swing. Their new album played on the speakers as Savanah leaned against the bar, surveying all that she had put together. Everyone was raving about the food and cocktail menu; the band was being led by their agent from table to table mingling with all the guests. A few times they had been pulled aside for interviews and had periodically found themselves in the social media corner, having their picture taken with the guests. Merchandise was selling out fast and everyone appeared to be having an incredible time. A satisfaction swelled in Savanah's chest as she took it all in, a deep pride for a job well done.

Sylvio leaned towards her, resting his elbow on the corner of the bar. "This event is epic, Savanah. We do events here from time to time and I know a lot of other local business owners that could use your services. Do you have business cards?"

"Yes!" Savanah replied, brightly reaching into her clutch and handing him a small stack.

"Thanks." he said, slipping them under the bar and bringing his eyes back to her. "You know, Savanah, you may be the best thing that ever happened to those guys, especially Rami."

"He's a good friend," Savanah replied, glancing over to where Rami was talking with a well-known local radio DJ.

"Friend?" Sylvio asked, a puzzled look washing over his handsome face.

"Yeah, we broke up in January." she shared, looking at her hands for a moment, then meeting his gaze.

"Ah, I see," he replied, looking towards Rami before continuing with a question. "Can I give you a piece of advice?" She nodded. "As a bartender, I see and hear a lot of things and witness the beginning and end of a lot of relationships. I inadvertently have a front row seat to a lot of drama. One thing I can tell you by watching your relationship with Rami is that the way he looks at you, well, it's the real deal. That guy over there..." he said, gesturing over to Rami. "...is head over heels in love with you and trust me when I say this, that kind of love isn't easy to find."

Savanah looked up into Sylvio's eyes and he gave her a knowing shrug as he made his way down the bar to take an order from a guest. Savanah glanced over to Rami, who met her gaze across the room, his eyes warming as he flashed her his gorgeous smile. A smile that made her heart do a flip flop. *Is Sylvio right? Is Rami still in love with me? Am I still in love with him?* Too many questions were clouding her mind as her head and heart continued to battle, her heart slowly winning out.

THE BAND PLAYED their first single and a short set of their new songs from their album, each one more amazing than the next. The buzz around the event, both there and on social media, was like an explosion with their hashtag already trending. Unquestionably, the event was a success.

"Hi" Rami said, sneaking up on Savanah who was over by the social media corner chatting with Dee and a couple of other guests.

She turned to him, her face incandescent in the dim light. "Hi." she replied, giving him a hip bump and taking a sip from her Pink Lady cocktail. He had to clench his hands to not reach out and wrap them around her, his desire to touch her palpable. "You, Savanah Smithfield, are remarkable," he complimented. "And I know when you first came in earlier tonight, I didn't say anything, but you may be the hottest woman I have ever laid eyes on in this outfit," he declared boldly, his eyes roaming over her head to toe.

She giggled, shimmying her hips, then striking a pose. The usual quieter Savanah was replaced by a slightly tipsy one, and he couldn't help but smile. *She is so crazy cute like this.* "No, I think you, Mr. Rockstar, are the remarkable one." She said, leaning in close and whispering into his ear, her warm raspberry and coconut scented breath on his cheek.

Rami smirked and leaned into her, planting a lingering kiss on her cheek. The softness of her skin, like home to his lips. She took half a step back, their eyes locking on each other as a raw heat passed between them. *It would be so easy to lean in and kiss her right now. To pull her into me.* She cleared her throat and offered him a smile as she asked, "Would you like to make the rounds with me?"

"Sure." he replied, as he bent his arm, offering it to her. Savanah took it and he beamed at her as they walked around the room arm in arm, mingling, talking, and laughing with the guests. Rami introduced her and she, with all the grace and charisma she possessed, handed out her business cards, everyone complimenting the event and praising her on a job well done. Spending the rest of the evening together, he couldn't help but feel immensely proud of her. *My Savanah is a rockstar too.*

With the amazing evening now over and everything cleaned up, Savanah thanked Sylvio and said her goodbyes, then exited the bar. When she made her way out the front door, Rami was parked there, leaning against his car, looking beyond sexy, with his long legs casually crossed at the ankles. She had been watching him all night, but seeing him with the moon capturing the glint in his gorgeous brown eyes, she felt her heart jolt at the sight of him.

"Need a ride home?" he asked, giving her his sweet smile. "I overhead you saying you were going to call a cab."

"Yeah, I was, but sure. Thank you."

He opened the passenger side door, and she offered him an appreciative smile. Climbing into the car, he glanced over at her, and he put his hand out to her in an offering. She glanced at it a moment and slipped her hand in his. The tender warmth of his touch made the incoming tide of emotion rise within her. She glanced at him, seeing all the love they once shared blazed across his handsome face. Not only a romantic love or a lustful love, which was undoubtedly still there, but a deep abiding love and adoration. A look that told her she was his every-thing. "Let's get you home," he roughly rasped before putting the car into drive.

They were quiet the entire drive home, the words unspoken hanging in the air, waiting to be said. He pulled into her driveway and put the car in park, then lay his head back on the headrest, turning his head to meet her eyes. She mimicked him, as she met his gaze and said, "Rami, I'm so sorry."

He popped his head up, furrowing his brows together in confusion as he insisted in a rush of words, "You have nothing to be sorry about, Savanah. I'm the one that screwed up our relationship."

"We both played a part, Rami. I jumped to conclusions that night. I was the insecure one, the one that was ques-tioning things. I was the one that was feeling insecure about us."

"But I was the one that made you feel insecure by putting you last," he added, insisting that she not take the blame for their relationship's demise.

"We both made mistakes," she conceded, as she glanced at her front door, not wanting this breakthrough in conversation to end. "Do you want to come inside to talk? I just want to spend some time with you. I know it's late, but..."

"I would like that," he interrupted, squeezing her hand.

They exited the car together, Savanah unlocking her door and leading him inside. Both climbed the stairs to the main floor in silence. Savanah set down her keys and removed her jacket, leaving her in just the bustier leather catsuit. "Mind if I change into something more comfortable? I know I'm owning this outfit, but my pajamas are calling my name right now."

"Go ahead." He said, a grin curling his lips as he took a seat at her island.

Savanah made her way down the hall and closed her bedroom door, leaning her body against it for a moment, closing her eyes. Tonight could be a turning point for them, and they had only scratched the surface of what they needed to discuss. Now if she could just tamp down her desire for him. That feeling he evoked in her that made her crave his kisses and touch. Rami had the ability to break down the wall she had built up, and him just being here in her home was already starting to make that wall crumble. She took a deep breath and went about changing into her favorite pair of pajamas. She entered her ensuite and washed the makeup off her face. Standing in front of the mirror, the memory of her first night with Rami, the night they simply slept together, came back to her in a rush. How he traced the freckles on her face and played with her hair, and how giving into exploration, he ran his hands over her body with reverence. As good as sex was between them, that night, with its tension and intensity, was the most intimate moment she had ever experienced. He made her feel truly coveted and seen for the first time in her life. She wanted that again with Rami, perhaps tonight. A decision forming, she exited the bedroom and found him. His head hung low in his hands, his fingers threaded through his hair and his shoulders shaking. She stopped, taking him in, and the tightening of emotion constricting her throat, sucking the breath from her lungs. "Rami, are you okay?" she whispered.

Rami's slowly lifted gaze, turning his face to her, his beautiful brown eyes red rimmed and puffy, his cheeks wet with salty tears. The realization that he had been crying caused a deep cavernous hole to bore into her chest. "I'm not okay." he answered the words coming out rough and tortured. "Tonight was probably one of the best nights of my career as a musician and still it doesn't come close to the night I kissed you on that dock. It doesn't even come close to topping the night when I saw you in the audience and realized you were my Savanah. It can't even measure up to the moment I realized I was hopelessly in love with you, and it will never hold a candle to the night I first made love to you," he rasped, an excruciating ache edging his voice. He turned his stool completely to face her his anguished eyes imploring hers. "All the fame, notoriety and accolades in the world will never be more important than you are to me. I could become the biggest rockstar in the world and none of it would matter if I don't have you by my side," he confessed, his words coming out in a rush as he blinked, and more tears spilled over onto his cheeks. "Don't you see? Without you, nothing else matters. You are my everything, Savanah."

Savanah felt the tears that had been welling up with his words overflow and trail down her cheeks with his declaration to her. All the pent-up emotions of the past nine months coming out like an undertow threatening to pull her in. She approached him slowly. He had turned away again, his head downcast, his shoulders shaking from the onslaught of tears. She slid her arms around him from behind, her face at his ear as he gripped her hands tight to his chest. They cried together, needing to let go of all the hurt they both held inside.

"I love you, Rami." Savanah whispered in his ear. "I never stopped, and I never will."

He lifted his head, swiveling the stool around, and pulled her into him so she was seated on his lap, and he was cradling her body. "I love you too, Savanah, more than anything in this world."

"Stay with me tonight. We can talk and figure this out and we can hold each other. I need to feel you close to me again. I've missed you so much." She confessed, caressing his cheek, wiping the tears away with affection.

He nodded, rising from the stool, still holding her in his arms. He carried her down the hall to her bedroom, coming around her side and setting her down on her feet gently. He cupped her face with one large hand, his sorrowful eyes looking straight into her soul as he whispered, his voice edging with emotion. "I just need a few minutes." Letting her go, she watched as he strode towards the ensuite, closing the door behind him.

Rami stood in front of the mirror, his face red and contorted from his tears. He was so tired, so exhausted from this painful ache in his heart. He lifted his shirt over his head and unbuckled his jeans, sliding them off. He stood there a minute with his hands resting on the counter, palms down, closing his eyes and breathing in and out slowly, trying to steady his racing heart. He could never remember a time where he broke down like that. Even after they broke up, and the overwhelming need to cry surfaced, he would never let himself simply pushing down the onslaught of emotions threatening to escape. Tonight, as he walked around the room with Savanah on his arm, them feeling like a couple again, he could feel the floodgates slowly open. Every bit of pain, guilt, and disappointment at how they ended crashed over him like a wave threatening to drown him.

Turning the faucet on, he splashed water on his face, letting it wash the remnants of his tears away. Meeting his red, puffy eyes in the mirror, his expression raw and vulnerable, he took one last calming breath and turned to the door. When he walked out, they were going to talk, truly talk about them and where to go from here. He was being given a chance to make things right, and he wasn't about to squander it. Rami picked up his discarded clothes and opened the door to find Savanah in bed, leaning against the headboard, her hands nervously wringing on her lap. She reached over and flipped the covers, inviting him to climb in next to her. The memory of the late night talks they had in this bed, the times they laughed and kissed and made love swirled around him. Resting his head back on the headboard, he turned his head to face her. She did the same, letting him speak first.

"First of all, I need you to know that night at the New Year's concert, I didn't cheat on you. The thought that you even considered that I would do that to you makes me sick to my stomach," he said, swallowing down hard.

"Layne and I were exiting the backstage door when some girls slipped past us, distracting the security. We were completely barricaded by fans and there was no security on us, as we tried to fulfil their demands for autographs and pictures. It was extremely overwhelming, as we had never had that kind of fanfare before." Savanah nodded, reaching for his hand as he went on. "The girl you saw with her hands and lips on me completely took me by surprise. Yes, I talked to her, but then she grabbed onto me and before I knew it, she was kissing me. I didn't have a chance to even think or process what was happening. I was in complete shock. I need you to know I never kissed her back," he explained, pinning her with his stare. "When she finally let go of me, you were there with a look of utter hurt and betrayal on your face. I knew how bad it looked and I tried to push her away Savanah, I swear to you I did. I would never do that to you. I would never be unfaithful to you."

Savanah smoothed her other hand over the one she was holding and raised her eyes to meet his. "I know you would never intentionally do that to me," she replied, as she gulped down, trying to steady her words as she explained. "When I saw that woman kiss you, it was a breaking point for me. I was feeling insecure about us long before that moment. You were on the cusp of a career that I knew had the potential to take you away from me, and I already felt like it was happening. I saw you being thrown into a lifestyle that is crazy and out of control. A lifestyle where people can take what they want from you, and you must accept it. Kind of like how that girl just took what she wanted from you without asking. I walked away from that lifestyle before and took control of my life, creating a bubble around myself that made me feel safe and secure. Being with you brought on that discomfort I once felt and I didn't want to lose you to all the craziness, like I almost lost myself."

"I don't even know what to say to that," he confessed, his brows drawing together with concern. "I don't think I can promise you I'll have a perfect balance between my career and us. But what I can promise you is that you won't lose me to the craziness. I will always try to put you first, Savanah. Although I want to have success with my band, if you tell me it's all too much and you don't want it anymore, I will walk away from it. The band and all the fanfare. I would give it all up for you. You are that important to me, Savanah."

Savanah searched his eyes to be met with complete candor. "I could never ask you to give up on your dream."

"I know you wouldn't, but I need you to know that you are far more important to me than the success. Being with you and loving you is all I want. Without that, like I said before, nothing else matters."

"I need you to know that I will never ask you to give up the band. I will not be a Yoko Ono." she said with a smile.

Rami let out a little chuckle at her Beatles reference, and his face turned serious again. "If the Band and I get a tour, which could likely happen in the next year, it may mean that we'll not be able to see each other for a while. Are you going to trust that I'm 100% completely committed to you and to us? Will you trust me when I say that I'm not going to get lost in all the craziness and hoopla?"

Savanah brought her hand up, caressing his cheek with tenderness, "Yes, I'll trust you, and I promise that if I feel insecure again about us, I'll tell you."

"Good," he replied, a hopeful smile tugging at his lips. "That's all I want. We need to communicate."

"Is there anything else you want?" she asked, sliding down to rest her head on the pillow, then looking up at him through her long lashes.

"Yes, I want to kiss you right now and make up for the time we lost."

Savanah's eyes turned dreamy as she reached for him. He hovered a moment, his lips a breath away from hers, their breaths mingling, hot and heady. Blinding love and lust beamed up at him as he bridged the gap and captured her lips. As they embraced, the last remnants of the hurt and pain vanished, allowing only their deep abiding love and a mutual understanding to remain.

SAVANAH WOKE the next morning feeling Rami's soft lips on her neck and shoulder. They had stayed up until the early hours of the morning, talking, kissing, and holding each other, but had not yet rekindled the intimacy they once shared. Of course, it wasn't for a lack of wanting to. Savanah wanted Rami to her core and knew that the makeup sex between them would be incredible. However, the emotional exhaustion of last night overrode their desires, and they both fell asleep in each other's arms.

Now, though, well rested and feeling that delectable tingle that was building within her, she saw no reason to hold back from what she wanted. She turned her body, meeting his brown eyes, hooded with desire, and pushed him back onto the mattress, taking him by surprise.

She kissed him passionately, straddling his strong lean body, her hands on his chest, as she rocked her core against his hardness, making him groan against her ravenous lips.

"Savanah." he groaned again as she trailed kisses down his neck, and across his chest, sliding down his body, branding over his taut stomach, her tongue tracing his abs. He sucked in a breath as she teased the V at his hips with her tongue. Hooking her fingers into the waist of his briefs, she slowly slid them down, his hips raising off the bed to help her. His hard member sprung free from its confines, and she licked her lips, taking in the hard, thick steel of him. She glanced up, their gazes locked, his breaths coming out laboured in anticipation. Her eyes not leaving his, she lowered her mouth and swirled her tongue around the head of him, capturing the moisture on the tip.

"Fuck." Rami growled, his entire body tensing as she took him deep.

The feeling of power that going down on him gave her, made her grow wet and the familiar ache to be filled by him consumed her. He closed his eyes and tilted his head back; lost in the pleasure she was eliciting as she devoured his length again and again. She moaned around his flesh; the vibrations causing him to jerk his head up and let out a low, deep growl of appreciation. "Keep doing that," he panted as she hummed around him. The vibration causing him to throw his head back on the pillow, closing his eyes as he stilled and spilled into her warm, willing mouth. She drank him in, lapping up every drop of his arousal before crawling back over him. Straddling his hips, she smiled at his reaction, letting out a naughty giggle. "Are you okay?"

Rami opened his eyes, a hazy look of satisfaction on his face as he gripped her hips.

"Yeah, damn, that was..." he started, bringing his hands to his head, and mimicking his mind being blown. Savanah smiled down at him and reached for the buttons of her nightshirt, slowly sensually unbuttoning them to reveal her bare breasts within. His darkened gaze flashed with desire as she slid the shirt off, tossing it to the floor, and brought his large palms to her breasts, teasing and massaging the sensitive swells and circling his thumbs over the peaks. She threw her head back, relishing the sensations as she ground her core over his. He hardened beneath her and growled, grabbing her around the waist as, with one swift move, he flipped her onto her back, making her eyes grow wide with surprise. "I need to feel all of you," he ground out, pressing her into the mattress. Sitting up, he hooked his fingers in the waistband of her pajama bottoms and panties and slid them down her long legs, tossing them to the side. "Protection?" he rasped out, meeting her gaze.

"I'm on birth control now, and you're the only one. I'm okay without, if you are," she replied, her eyes a blazing inferno of raw lust and need.

"There has only been you," he replied, covering her body with his, his eyes searching hers. "Are you sure?"

"Yes, I want nothing between us," her request, more poignant now than ever before.

Raising his hips, he slid into her body, making her gasp in pleasure, feeling the familiar stretch but now more intense with no barrier between them.

"Oh, my God." he groaned as he pressed into her fully. "You feel so good."

"So, do you." She panted as he pulled back and thrust back into her, pressing deep. He did it again, making her cry out with pleasure, her body overly sensitized with the bare contact. Finding their cadence, he took her in long, deep strokes, lifting her legs over his shoulders, allowing him to go deeper, as he thrust into her unrelentingly, bringing them higher. Their bodies covered in a sheen of sweat. He pressed into her one more time, and she shattered, her walls clenching as white-hot pleasure ripped through her body like a storm. She cried out, his name on her lips as her orgasm consumed her, swallowing her whole. He thrust once, twice, and on the third, let out a guttural growl as he joined her in sweet release. Barely holding his hard body up, he lowered her legs and kissed her sensually as their breaths came out ragged against each other's lips. Smoothing his hair from his eyes, she searched them, pure, honest, and true love in their depths. "I love you so much, Savanah." he choked out. "I've missed this. I've missed us. I'm never letting you go again."

She smiled, her heart bursting with love for this man. "I'm here, Rami. I'm all yours." She replied, kissing him passionately with a promise that this time there was nothing that could come between them.

CHAPTER 14

To say that Prairie Sound had found success was an understatement. In the following months since the release of their first album, their first single skyrocketed on the Canadian charts. They signed a record deal for a well-respected label that had launched the careers of some of their musical idols. They were picked up as an opening act for Aerosmith's North American tour starting at the beginning of January and as their following grew; they were being touted as one of the hottest up and coming rock groups to come out of Canada.

As for Savanah, her business was booming. She was booked solid that holiday season for corporate parties and booked three more weddings in the coming year. She was quickly becoming the person to go to for all the parties and events in the area. Although their lives were probably the busiest they had ever been, they had found a routine and a balance between work and their relationship. It wasn't perfect, but with a newfound trust and understanding, they were figuring it out together and, more importantly; they were communicating openly and honestly.

Now, with another Christmas upon them, they were both determined to change the narrative of the year before and make this Christmas truly special.

Rami and Savanah walked back to her townhome from another amazing Perez Navidad celebration, both a little tipsy. It was the early hours of Christmas morning, and the night was cold and crisp with big fluffy snowflakes drifting down from the sky, blanketing everything in pristine white. It was like walking in a winter wonderland, magical and sparkling. Rami had his arm draped over Savanah and his guitar in its case in his other hand. Savanah pulled the crocheted toque on her head down over her ears and put her mittened hand out to capture some snowflakes.

"I love nights like this," she mused, looking up, white flakes sticking to her long lashes.

Rami laughed and turned her to face him. Then he leaned down, kissing her eyelids, making her giggle. "Did I ever tell you how cute you are when you drink?"

She hooked her arms around his neck and planted a chaste kiss on his lips, the taste of lime lingering when she pulled away. "Marnie makes a killer Margarita." she purred as she released him and reached down, gathering some snow with her mittens. She turned to Rami, her eyes twinkling with mischief in the streetlight. Cupping the snow, she formed it into a ball and threw it at him, smacking him square in the chest. Rami blinked at her, his brow cocked in challenge as he leaned down, set down his guitar case and scooped up some snow prepping his retaliation. She threw him a taunting look and teased, "Come and get me."

He threw the snowball, hitting her back as she turned. She giggled and caught her boot on a small patch of ice, making her lose her balance and fall into a drift of freshly fallen snow. Rami rushed to her side, and she pulled him into the drift with her, both now laughing as they lay there on the edge of someone's front yard surrounded by cold wetness.

Rami turned his head to face Savanah, her cheeks and nose a bright pink and her blue eyes dancing with delight, thinking there was no one he wanted to experience these little moments with more.

* * *

AFTER THEIR SNOWY WALK HOME, Savanah fixed them each a cup of hot chocolate and they settled on the couch, Savanah's legs resting on his lap as they sipped their hot chocolate and stared at the Douglas fir in the corner, the multicolored lights twinkling in the darkened living room. A contented quiet surrounding them.

They sat there together for a long time, until Savanah broke the silence, a look of blissful contentment on her face. "I can see us ten years from now, just like this. Our kids fast asleep in their beds, dreaming about what Santa Claus will bring them and you and I enjoying the quiet after setting all the gifts under the tree. Just a time for us to enjoy the peace and stillness before the storm of excitement that comes on Christmas morning." She said dreamily, her eyes drifting from the tree to meet his eyes, a rosy hue blooming on her cheeks. "Sorry, I guess it's weird to be thinking about the future like that. We just got back together, and..."

"I think about those kinds of things too," he reassured her, with so much love in his eyes it was blinding. "When I think of the future, I always think of you in it. I can see doing everything with you."

Curling up her nose as she asked, "So, it doesn't scare you when I talk about our kids, where I would like to live, or about our future?"

He shook his head and laughed, "Nope, I want 2 to 4 kids and I would love to buy a house in Primrose."

Savanah's eyes widened, and a slow smile curled her lips. "I like Primrose." she said, resting her head on the couch. "It would be nice to be close to Garrett, Bea and Amelia and you could be close to Marnie. I can work from anywhere now and I like the idea of a small town and raising our kids there. Sounds perfect to me."

* * *

THE NEXT MORNING SAVANAH WOKE, her head resting on Rami's chest, her body curled around his. She was always so cold, so she loved having him as her own personal source of heat. She could lie here all day like this, but her body protested, so she rolled over to slip away to the bathroom. But before she could steal away, Rami pulled her back flush with his body, burrowing his face in her hair, making her squirm.

"I need to pee," she giggled as he released her and he

groaned, reaching for her as she strode into the ensuite, closing the door. "What time is it?" she called out.

"10:36 a.m.!" he shouted from behind the closed door.

"We have our Christmas lunch at Garrett and Bea's at noon, so I'm going to take a quick shower!"

Stripping out of her pajamas, she stepped into the bathtub, closing the curtain behind her. She turned the water on, adjusting it to her preference, when the curtain suddenly opened, startling her. Rami stood there in all his hot and sexy naked glory, and she raised a brow in question. "Are you joining me?"

"I was getting lonely and cold in bed without you," he said, climbing in, closed the curtain and gripped her hips. She leaned down to flick the shower head on and he growled as her behind brushed his groin.

"Sorry, there's not a lot of space."

"Oh, there's enough space." he growled in her ear, bringing her back to his front, feeling his body harden between them. "Enough space to do all the naughty things I want to do to you."

"Rami." she giggled as the water trailed down their bodies and he massaged her breasts, teasing their peaks. She loved when he did that, the sensations going straight to her core, making her let out a raspy moan. "Baby, we need to shower and get ready for lunch."

"It's more fun to get clean once you've gotten a little dirty," he growled, sliding one hand down her stomach to her apex, circling the centre of her with his fingers. She panted in response as he ordered, his breath hot against her ear. "Lean forward and palms against the wall."

She complied as he smoothed his hand down her back,

giving him a perfect angle to plunge into her. She cried out with pleasure as he filled her completely, hitting the coveted spot, sparking delicious sensations in her core. He withdrew and took her again and again, the sounds of their moans and hot wet skin making contact echoing off the tile walls of the confined space. The familiar build of her orgasm grew as he reached between her legs, strumming the bundle of nerves feverishly until her body vibrated, her inner walls gripping as wave after wave of pleasure took over. Rami stilled, a feral growl escaping his lips as his release peaked. Slipping out of her, he brought her body flush with his and held her close as they caught their breaths under the spray.

Planting kisses along the column of her neck, he whispered. "Sorry to interrupt your shower."

Savanah turned, bringing her lips to his in a scorching kiss, causing him to back into the tile wall as she pressed her body to his. She released their kiss and looked up at him through her long lashes with a coy grin. "You are welcome in the shower with me anytime." He started to harden with the press of her body and her open invitation, and she giggled, turning around to adjust the spray. "Oh no you don't, we're going to be late."

LATER THAT DAY at Garrett and Bea's house, after their delicious traditional Irish lunch and what seemed like mountains of gifts to open, Rami went into the kitchen to get himself and Savanah a soda. Bryan, Savanah's dad, entered the kitchen and offered Rami a tentative smile.

"Do you have a moment to talk?" he asked, clapping Rami on the back.

Rami looked at him with surprise. This was only the second time he had met Savanah's dad and the last time he didn't seem to approve of him. "Yes... of course," he replied hesitantly as he followed Bryan into the hallway.

Bryan's eyes were downcast a moment and when he looked up, he was met with regret in their depths. "I just wanted to apologize for last year when we first met. I came across very critical about your relationship with my daughter and about your band."

"Oh, I... it's fine." Rami stuttered, taken aback by her father's candor.

"No, it's not. I know my opinion likely played a part in breaking you and Savanah up. I put doubt in my daughter's head and that was wrong of me," he admitted, his voice edging with guilt. "I was being overprotective and treating her like my little girl and not like the grown woman she is. I know how devastated Savanah was when you two broke up and I could see how much you loved each other. Now I can see how happy you make my daughter and that's all I want for her. To be happy."

"I love her very much, Bryan. She's it for me." Rami confessed, feeling emboldened by her father's apology to him. "I want to marry her someday."

Her father met Rami's eyes and offered him a warm, kind smile. "Well, know when the time is right to ask her. You have my blessing. And please start calling me Dad. You're part of our family now."

Emotion rose to the surface, threatening to overflow as Rami took in her father's approval. No words quite adequate to describe how honored his acceptance made him feel.

Garrett strode up slowly to them, an apprehensive look on his face. "Is everything alright over here?"

Bryan cleared his throat, the emotion of their exchange affecting him too. "Yes, yes, Rami here was just about to tell me about his band's upcoming tour with Aerosmith."

"You used to love that band. Haven't you seen them in concert like eight times?" Garrett shared with a laugh as he eyed his father.

Rami's eyes widened, and a smirk curved his lips as he said, "You've been holding out on me, Dad."

RAMI AND SAVANAH pulled into the driveway of the townhome and made their way inside.

"Why are Christmas festivities so exhausting?" Savanah asked, trudging up the stairs to her main floor, her hands full of bags and boxes. Setting everything down on the table, Rami followed her with his hands full, too. "Was that everything?"

"Yes." he replied. "We can clean this all up tomorrow. I have something special for you."

"Rami." Savanah tilted her head, giving him a chiding look. "We agreed we wouldn't give each other anything this year."

"I didn't go shopping, but you never said anything about homemade gifts," he replied as he took her hand and led her to the couch.

He reached for his guitar case, snapping it open and pulling out his guitar. Taking a seat on the chair facing her, he asked, "Remember when you and I were seated at the piano before Garrett and Bea's wedding, and I started to play a song for you?"

"Yes, it was so beautiful, and you said it was something you were working on." She answered brightly, the memory coming back to her.

"What you heard that day was the beginning of a love song," he replied, his eyes so soft and tender as he asked, "Can I sing what I have so far?"

Savanah nodded and beamed with pure excitement as he started to play, his fingers adeptly strumming the guitar as he looked up at her, his eyes locked on hers as he sang her the song.

Warm summer nights beneath the stars
You captured my attention, woke up my young heart.
Your beauty brighter than the moon above
I felt the stirrings, the beginnings of love.
Because I knew without a doubt that I couldn't live without you in my life
You are my first, you are my last
You are my everything.
You are my present; you are my past.
You are my everything.
When the hands of time had passed,
You manifested for me at last.
All the feelings I had before now making sense.
The more time I spent with you, I knew our love was pure and true.

Because I knew without a doubt that I couldn't live without you in my life.

You are my first, you are my last
You are my everything.
You are my present; you are my past.
You are my everything.

HE STOPPED, his hands stilling on his guitar. She smiled as a tear rolled down her cheek and she swiped it away with her hand. "It's a work in progress. I need one last verse to complete it, but I wanted you to hear it first." he confessed, lifting the guitar over his head, and setting it back in its case.

She rose from the couch and rounded the coffee table, climbing onto his lap. Wrapping her arms around his neck, she met his gaze, reflecting the love in his eyes. "That was the best Christmas gift I could ever get. I loved it."

Rami brushed his lips to hers, soft and tender as he declared. "You are my everything, Savanah."

She smoothed her hand over his face tenderly and planted another chaste kiss on his lips before she climbed off his lap and reached into the tree pulling out a little box wrapped nicely with a red bow as she confessed, "I have a little gift for you too." Rami gave her a look of surprise and cocked his brow at her shaking his head. "Don't worry, I didn't go shopping either and it's sort of home-made, or I had it made," she explained with a smile as she handed it to him and curled back into his lap.

He unwrapped it and glanced up at her expectant gaze.

Opening the little box, he found a key inside. Holding it up, he gave her a puzzled look.

"It's your own key to this house. My house, and I was hoping soon, our house."

He looked at her for a moment, as he processed, the spark of realization flashing in his eyes as he asked, "You want me to move in with you?"

She nodded and continued, her gaze sincere and tender, "I want you to live here with me and I was hoping I could be your home. That you always know that no matter where you and the band go, that I'm right here waiting for you and always will be."

Taking her face in his hands, his eyes glinting with joy, he replied. "Savanah, yes, I will move in. Wherever you are is where I want to be."

* * *

THE NEXT WEEK Rami moved into the townhouse, Prairie Sound prepared and practiced for the upcoming tour, and Rami and Savanah spent every moment they could with each other until the day arrived for the band to leave for the tour. 30 cities in 75 days, their first show in St. Paul, Minnesota. Having rented a small tour bus with enough room for all their equipment, luggage and more, Rex pulled into the driveway of Layne's house and pressed the horn. Rex may be the wild and crazy drummer of Prairie Sound, but with his family owning a large trucking company in St. Augustine, he was licensed and certified to drive just about anything. Steve climbed out of the bus, followed by Rex rounding the front of the vehicle, his heavy combat boots crunching on the snowy driveway.

"Hey there, pink lady!" Rex greeted loudly, seeing Savanah. "Here to give me a kiss goodbye?" he teased, puckering up his lips.

Savanah, having grown used to Rex and his flirtations, gave him a "not a chance" look and giggled. Despite Rex's tough exterior, Rex Johnson was truly an awesome guy, and she couldn't help but like him and his surly ways.

"Get your own girl." Rami responded playfully, wrapping his arms around Savanah from behind, holding onto her possessively.

Rex held up his hands and gave Savanah a wink, making her smile at his rakish brand of charm.

The band loaded up the rest of the luggage and turned to Rami and Savanah.

"Let's let these two lovebirds say their goodbyes." Layne offered, flashing them a knowing smile.

Rami's face turned serious as he gave his friend a look of thanks. Layne nodded, and the band loaded onto the bus. Rami turned to Savanah, his eyes glistening with sadness as he met her gaze. Savanah had spent a lot of time over the last week mentally preparing herself for their goodbye and tried to steady her emotions in this moment. Seeing him look so sad, it couldn't help but break her resolve.

"Facetime me when you get there?" Savanah reminded, wrapping her arms around his neck.

"And every day we'll either video chat, talk on the phone or text." Rami added with reassurance as he reached up to cup her cheek and look deep into her eyes. "I want you to know I'll come back the same guy that left."

She searched his eyes, feeling his emotions, a combination of wariness and fear in their depths. *Is he scared to go with fear that I would become insecure again? I need him to know we'll be okay.*

"I trust you Rami. I'll be right here waiting for you when you get back. I'm not going anywhere." He let out a long exhale, a look of relief washing over his face. "I love you, baby, and always will."

He captured her lips with his in a tender kiss that quickly became deep and passionate, as their tongues tangled and he lifted her into his arms, her legs wrapping around his lean body.

Cheers and catcalls sounded from the bus, and they turned to see all the guys peering at them through the windows with their thumbs up.

"I guess that's my cue to go." Rami laughed, Savanah giggling into his neck. She raised her face to meet his eyes, the love and promise in them making a lump form in her throat. "You are my everything Savanah, I love you with all my heart." He gave her one more breathless kiss before he set her onto her feet and reached down to pick up his guitar case. His other hand in hers, he let it go and strode over to the bus, looked back at her over his shoulder with his heart-stopping smile, then got into the bus and closed the door. Savanah waved as the bus pulled out of the driveway and disappeared down the road, already missing him.

CHAPTER 15

Savanah entered Everything you Knead to be greeted by the most glorious smell of melted butter, brown sugar, and cinnamon. Marnie's bright and beautiful face welcomed her from behind the counter. "Savanah!"

Marnie came around and wrapped her in a big hug. She and Marnie had become close over the past few months and while Rami was away on tour, she had tried to come around to spend some time with her and had even brought her to a few Sunday family dinners. Having gone through a difficult time recently, Savanah so appreciated that Marnie even thought of her.

"You popped in on a good day! I have fresh cinnamon buns just out of the oven." She shared, making her voice sing song.

"That's why I'm here!" Savanah exclaimed.

A voice called Savanah's name from the corner of the bakery and a head of fiery curls that could only belong to Bea, popped up with her hand up in greeting.

Savanah smiled and waved back as Marnie went behind the counter to plate her a fresh cinnamon bun. She strode over to the table, to be met by Bea, Whitney and Ever's bright and shiny faces.

"Hello ladies! Thank you for the invitation to join you." she said, taking a seat next to Ever.

Ever put her arm around her, giving her a squeeze. "I haven't seen you in forever. Not since last summer, just before you shut down Pretty Things."

"That's right, yikes! It's been a while. I've been so busy lately, with my new business Pink Lady Productions and with..."

"With a certain rockstar." Whitney interrupted, a grin curling her lips as she wiggled her eyebrows. "I heard you two are living together now."

"Yeah, well, technically, and we will be once he's back from touring this spring." She explained. "He moved in and then left a few days later on tour."

They all nodded their heads and Marnie appeared with a plated cinnamon bun and a coffee pot in hand. Setting the cinnamon bun in front of Savanah,, she poured coffee into everyone's mugs and turned to her, glancing down at her plate. Savanah's eyes darted around the table to see everyone was watching her intently.

"Ah, do I have something on my face?" she asked, touching her face and giggling.

"No, but this is your first famous Primrose cinnamon bun experience. We want to know what you think." Bea laughed, gesturing for her to take a bite.

"You got to pick it up and get right in there." Ever added, urging her on.

Savanah giggled and obliged, picking up the cinnamon bun and inhaling the delicious, sweet smell. *When in Primrose.* She bit into the decadent confection and her eyes closed, as the heavenly combination of rich butter, caramelized brown sugar, spicy cinnamon, tender pastry and luscious cream cheese frosting captivated her senses and she audibly moaned. Everyone around the table laughed, clapping their hands, and cheering as Savanah looked up to Marnie with wide eyes, her mouth still full of the cinnamon goodness. She brought her hand up to cover her mouth as she mumbled through the bite, "This may be the best thing I ever put in my mouth." The entire group burst out with laughter as Savanah licked the frosting off her lips and reached for her napkin to wipe her mouth.

The door chime sounded, and Marnie rushed off to greet another customer. With rosy cheeks, Savanah glanced around the table at the wonderful women and realized how much she missed the daily social interaction her store gave her. An unfamiliar pang of longing to be part of a community such as Primrose overtook her. Rami had talked about one day wanting to settle in Primrose and sitting here with this circle of friends. She confirmed she wanted that, too.

* * *

THE PHRASE, "absence makes the heart grow fonder" was something Rami never thought twice about, but having been away from Savanah for the past two and a half months, he felt those words deep down in his soul.

Although they did a good job keeping in contact during the tour, nothing compared to having her in his arms.

Having dropped Layne and Steve off already, Rami felt the all-consuming desire to see Savanah and fidgeted in his seat restlessly. Rex glanced over at him, letting out a gruff laugh as he said, "Hang tight there, lover boy. We're almost there." Turning onto their street, Rex parked the bus in front of the townhouses and turned to Rami, putting out his hand. "It's been real, my friend."

Rami clasped his hand and pulled his bandmate and friend in for a hug. Although he spent a lot of time with his band before the tour, having spent every day for 2 ½ months traveling together throughout the US, performing in incredible venues, and simply sharing experiences, laughs and conversation, he had to admit he was feeling kind of sad that it was over.

"Go on, go see your girl," Rex said, releasing their embrace and clearing his throat, the emotion that it was over getting to him too.

Rami climbed into the back, retrieving his guitar and suitcases, and exited out the side. As Rex drove off, Rami swallowed down, trying to steady his emotions as he stared at the townhouse. "Home." he whispered. "Finally, home." He breathed in deeply and let out a long exhale as he made his way towards the front door and unlocked it.

Setting his guitar and suitcases down, he removed his combat boots and exclaimed, "Honey, I'm home!"

There was no reply. The townhome was eerily silent. Climbing the stairs, the main level was dark, except for a few jar candles on the island illuminating the space. Rami glanced around and spotted a note on the island. He picked it up, and it read:

Welcome home, you sexy rockstar. Come find me.

Rami grinned. Their place was small, so he glanced towards the hallway, seeing a faint glimmer of light coming from their bedroom. Entering the room slowly, he wasn't expecting to see what was in front of him. Sprawled seductively across the bed in nothing but a Prairie Sound T-shirt was Savanah looking like his every erotic dream. Her pink hair was pulled back in a sexy high ponytail, and the wide neck of the t-shirt draped down, exposing her bare shoulder. His eyes trailed over her body the length of the t-shirt, reaching high on her upper thigh revealing the sexy curve of her behind and the smooth expanse of her impossibly long legs.

"Welcome home." She purred, her voice raspy and sexy.

My girlfriend is a sex kitten. His lips curved up in a smile and he reached for the hem of his shirt, pulling it off in one swoop. Unbuckling his belt, she turned on her side, crooking her finger at him, beckoning him over. *Holy shit.* Instantly hard, he quickly removed the rest of his clothes and, naked, stalked up to the bed, crawled over her and hovered over her body, pinning her to the mattress. Savanah's eyes danced in the candlelight as he breathed her in, her sweet floral scent intoxicating him. "Hi" he whispered, flashing her a coquettish grin.

"Hi." she whispered back, running her fingers languidly over the slope of his taut back. "I've missed you."

She wrapped her legs around his back, hooking her ankles, as he captured her lips, kissing her hard and deep before replying against her lips, "I've missed you too." Then taking her in another scorching kiss. She moaned into his mouth., He lifted his head, needing to see her beautiful face.

"I've missed your eyes," he said, planting feathery kisses on her eyelids. "I've missed your nose and these gorgeous freckles." He said, kissing his way down the bridge of her nose. "I've missed these delicious lips." he continued capturing her lips again in a passionate kiss. "And I have missed your sexy body." he finished running his hand down her side, over her hip and gliding up one long leg.

Nestled between her legs, he ground his hard ridge over her drenched core, making her breath hitch with the sweet friction as she rasped, "Fuck me."

He didn't need to be asked twice. He lined himself up and sank into the heaven that was his girlfriend. Her eyes rolled back with a gasp of pleasure. The enrobing molten heat of her body inviting him in and pulsing around his length.

"Take me hard, Rami." she begged, her eyes wild with wanton lust. "I want it hard and fast."

As per her request, he claimed her with hard deep slides, the sound of their skin connecting along with her gasps, moans and cries of pleasure filling the room. With one more punishing thrust, they flew over the edge together, calling out each other's names as they crested. Collapsing on top of her, he buried his head in her neck, trying to catch his breath and he rolled onto his back, bringing her with him, their bodies still connected as she straddled him.

"I'm so happy you're home." She murmured, her eyes shining with blissed out happiness and satiation. She leaned in and kissed him hungrily, their tongues gliding together in a sensuous dance. A kiss to make up for all the lost kisses of the past few months. Before they drifted off to sleep in each other's arms, they made love again, this time slowly and tenderly, the emotion of being reunited filling their hearts with ardor.

SOME SAY that the moment you realize you want to spend the rest of your life with someone, it's like the world stops and you have this epiphany that they are the one. For Rami, he couldn't pinpoint the exact moment when it happened to him. It seemed to be a million different tiny moments that brought him to clarity. All the times she tucked her hair behind her ear when she was curled up on the couch reading. The countless nights she slid her cold feet against his warm calves, reminding him she was there. The moments she bit the corner of her lip when she was concentrating on something. Every single day when she looked at him, like he hung the moon. Each small, miniscule moment that culminated to him knowing beyond a shadow of a doubt that Savanah Smithfield was his forever.

Then, when his sister reunited with the love of her life, Davis Baxter, the brother of Bea and a career military man, with whom she shared a whirlwind relationship, quick engagement and married only two weeks later, he asked himself, *what are you waiting for?* Seeing the love that

Marnie and Davis shared, despite their circumstances, inspired Rami. He knew he had that kind of undying love and devotion with Savanah, and he wanted their future to start now. He just needed a little advice before he took that final step.

Rami entered the Eazy Café in Primrose, the smell of delicious bacon, eggs, toast, deep fried potatoes, and freshly brewed coffee permeated his senses. With it being a Saturday morning, the café was packed with locals getting their greasy breakfast fix. With many of the faces, regulars at the bakery, he was greeted with smiles, waves, and hellos as he made his way over to Garrett, who was seated at a booth in the back corner.

"Hey, man! Nice to see you!" Garrett said, getting up and giving him a brotherly hug.

Garrett had quickly become a close friend and mentor to Rami. Never having had a big brother, Rami appreciated his candor and advice, especially when it came to his sister and there was no one else he trusted more to keep his plans on the down low.

A waitress came over, pouring Rami some coffee and taking their breakfast orders. When she hurried off, Garrett leaned back in the booth and gave Rami a mischievous smile. "So, let me guess. You wanted to meet me here today because you're wanting to propose to Savanah."

Rami laughed in response, running his hand through his curly hair as he asked, "Am I that obvious?"

"No." Garrett answered as he leaned forward and rested his elbows on the table. "But I have been expecting it."

"Do you think it's too soon?" Rami asked, his brows raised in question.

"No, man. I knew I was going to marry Bea within months of dating and less than a year of knowing her I proposed." he shared, meeting his gaze. "When you know, you know."

"It's true. I can't say exactly when I knew she was the only one for me, but she is. Savanah is who I want to spend the rest of my life with."

Garrett smiled at his declaration and his gaze turned thoughtful as he said, "I read once that love begins as an emotion and over time it grows into a verb. It's little things, each day, either things she does, or things you do to show how much you love that other person. For me, it was how Bea helped and supported me through post traumatic stress from losing my first wife, Dani. How she showed such unconditional love to Amelia and how we could simply sit still together and feel completely happy and content. It was nothing huge or flashy. Just her being her, us living life together and simply knowing there was no one else I wanted to spend that life with."

Rami took in his words and smiled. "I can't imagine living life without Savanah."

"Then, Rami, you're ready." he grinned back as he clapped his hands together. "Now tell me what you have in mind for the proposal."

* * *

IT WAS A GORGEOUS SUMMER NIGHT, the light breeze a welcome reprieve as the sounds of the Summer Fair echoed off in the distance. Savanah was at the front of the crowd waiting for the concert to start, surrounded by her family, Rami's family, and all their closest friends. She looked around, taking in each person, feeling grateful for each one and thinking how amazing it was that they could all gather to support Prairie Sound as they headlined the Summer in the City Mainstage concerts.

As she waited for the stage lights to come up, she couldn't help but feel nostalgic, thinking back to two years ago when she saw Rami again after so many years. Seeing her once dear friend and teenage crush, now a gorgeous rockstar on stage, was surreal and when their eyes met, she knew her life would never be the same. The memory of that night came back, like waves lapping the shoreline. It felt like a lifetime ago, yet just like yesterday. Two years of loving him through every up and down, only to come out stronger in the end. Two of the best years of her life. He was her person, and she was his and there was no one else she could imagine doing life with.

The stage lights came up, and the crowd roared as Rami walked on stage, the raw edge of his electric guitar filling the open space, causing the anticipation to rise and adrenaline to pump wildly through the fans. Savanah felt her own pulse quicken as the spotlight brought her sexy as sin boyfriend into view. Dressed in a tight white V-neck t-shirt stretched over his taut torso, torn black jeans that sat low on his narrow hips, his signature combat boots and leather cuffs, he was every girl's rockstar dream and Savanah couldn't help but think, *he's all mine.*

The rest of the stage lights came up, revealing the rest of the band. Layne, Steve, and Rex, all ready to rock out as

Rami stepped to the microphone and started singing, his rich edgy voice bringing on another wave of screams from the crowd as he belted out their first hit single. Savanah looked to her left, her mom and dad beside her, big smiles on their faces and their eyes transfixed on Rami as he sang. Over the past few months, her parents had become very close to Rami. They had accepted him as part of the family and although she never knew exactly what transpired between her father and Rami last Christmas; she knew that was the transition point in his relationship with them. They loved him and, more importantly; they loved him for her. Looking to her right, she saw Rami's parents, Marnie, and all his younger brothers. Even his Abuela was there, her hands in the air, cheering loudly for her grandson. She thought about how intimidated she was when meeting them for the first time, but how incredibly warm and welcoming they had been. Now, having spent countless family dinners with them, she felt truly like a member of the Perez clan. Marnie caught her gaze and hooked her arm around her waist, giving her a squeeze.

"Are you good?" she asked.

"Just feeling so incredibly happy." Savanah replied, her eyes dancing with the glint of the stage lights. "Everyone is here."

"Because we love you both," Marnie replied, giving her a side hug.

Savanah glanced behind her to see Dee's smiling face and her brother Garrett, his blue eyes dancing as he had his arms around Bea protectively. He gestured with his chin to the stage and her eyes darted up to see Rami, his eyes transfixed on her. She smiled and gave him a wink, eliciting his sexy, lopsided smile as he continued to sing. *My god, I love him.*

The two-hour concert was incredible. With Prairie Sound delivering as only they could, they wound down the concert with another hard-hitting original and the band walked off the stage. The captivated crowd chanted, "Encore, encore, encore..."

The band reappeared, this time with Rami holding his acoustic guitar slung over his shoulder and a stool in hand. Steve followed, carrying another stool and set it next to the other one. Rami took a seat and adjusted the microphone as he smiled out at the crowd.

"Did you all have fun tonight, St. Augustine?" he shouted, the crowd responding with a roar. "We always love playing the fair and two years ago we were right here playing it for the first time when I saw a familiar face down in the front row. A face I hadn't seen in eight years, but one I could never forget. Someone I shared my first kiss with one beautiful night under the stars." The collective sound of swoony sighs washed over the crowd as he continued. "From that night, two years ago, I have been completely head over heels in love with my first kiss, my first crush and my first love, Mi amor Savanah." he said, meeting her gaze. "And I have a song I want to sing for you. Can you join me on stage, baby?"

Savanah looked around at all her family and friends, their eyes locked on her, their smiles wide and beaming. A security guard approached her, and she followed him as he guided her up a set of stairs to the stage. She walked on stage, to be met with a sea of happy faces and loud cheers.

She gave the crowd a wave and a smile as she glanced at Rami's handsome face, so full of love and adoration for her. She leaned down and kissed him chastely before she took a seat on the stool next to him.

Turning to the mic he said, "This is my girlfriend, Savanah, and I wrote this next song for her, because from that first kiss to our first I love you, and everything in between, she has become my everything. This song's for you, baby."

Savanah meet his eyes as he turned his body to face her and started strumming the familiar melody to their love song. Her breath hitched as the rest of the band joined in behind her, Steve on the keyboard enriching the sound, Layne taking on the bass and Rex keeping the beat of the beautiful ballad. Rami's eyes trained on hers as he began to sing their song, the beautiful lyrics sharing their love story. Two kids when they met, not knowing that they would end up here on this stage, so deeply in love. Rami went into the chorus talking about all their firsts they had shared, memories both past and present, carved so deep they had become part of their souls. By the second chorus the audience started singing along and Savanah turned, smiling out at the adoring fans before her eyes turned to Rami as he went into the last verse, words she hadn't heard before.

They say you will know

That the universe will show you when it's right

That the warmth of your embrace and the smile across your face

Will tell me now's the time to make you mine

Two years is all it took to bring me to one knee with just one look.

Because I know right here, right now, without a shadow of a doubt.

Rami rose from the stool, sliding his guitar around his back as the rest of the band carried the song into the chorus, the crowd singing along. *You are my first, you are my last, you are my everything...* and Savanah's eyes widened with the realization of what was happening. Rami dropped to one knee in front of their family, friends, his band and all their adoring fans and looked up at her, his eyes reflecting all the love he felt for her and more as he asked, "Savanah, Mi Amor, will you marry me?"

He pulled a ring box out of his back pocket and opened it to reveal the most beautiful pink diamond ring she had ever seen. She looked down to her family, seeing her mother and Bea hugging each other with tears in their eyes and over to her dad, his eyes glistening with emotion, a wide smile on his face as he gave her an approving nod. She looked down at the stunning ring and met Rami's beautiful brown eyes again, knowing he was her everything too.

"Yes!" she shouted above the swell of the music and the singing crowd. A roar erupted, her answer echoing through the audience as Rami got to his feet, and she jumped into his arms and wrapped her legs around his waist. She looked deep into his eyes, seeing her future, so bright and blinding as she brought her lips to his, kissing her now fiancé and not caring who was watching.

CHAPTER 16

The next year was filled with so many firsts. In fall, Prairie Sound was asked to join the European leg of a world tour for the Rolling Stones, and they were nominated for best new artist at the Juno awards. Savanah was nominated for a Canadian Entrepreneurship award and won. Rami and Savanah purchased their first home together, a beautiful two-story character home at the end of Main Street, Primrose with space for a home office for Savanah and a separate building that the band could renovate into a studio. Life had come full circle, and all that was left to do was get married.

As their family and friends gathered around the edge of Lake Clearwater, on a beautiful late afternoon the following August, a light breeze rustled the trees and sent ripples across the tranquil lake. Savanah looked out at the scene in front of her. The gorgeous archway cascaded with pink and white peonies, the white chairs on either side of the aisle sprinkled with pink rose petals and the impossibly handsome man at the end of the aisle, waiting anxiously for his bride. She smoothed down the pink tulle of her wedding dress and touched her hand to the bodice, the butterflies dancing in her belly.

"Are you ready?" her father asked, offering her a smile, pure joy on his face.

"Yes, dad, I'm ready."

* * *

THE MOMENT RAMI SAW HER, his breath caught as the most radiant woman in pink floated towards him. Her dress with a fitted bodice of delicate lace cut in a sweetheart neckline, showing her gorgeous shoulders and flawless skin. Flutter sleeves draped off her shoulders in tulle and the long tulle skirt gave the illusion like she was walking on air. Her makeup was light, letting her natural glow come through, and her pink hair was brought up at the sides, cascading in luscious thick waves down her back. *This is what an angel looks like. Mi amor, my Savanah.*

Reaching the end of the aisle, Savanah's beautiful blue eyes met Rami's, and he felt the emotion bubble to the surface. "You look amazing," he whispered.

She smiled with boundless love in her gaze as she replied. "You too."

Rami smoothed his hands over the lapels of his custom suit and looked down at his feet to see his usual combat boots. Savanah followed his gaze and let out a knowing giggle as she shook her head.

Their minister stepped forward and asked, "Who gives this woman to this man?"

"Her mother and I do," her father replied as he leaned in and kissed Savanah on the cheek and with a smile, lay her hand in Rami's.

He glanced up at Rami, his eyes glossy with happiness and tears as he said, "Take care of my girl."

Rami nodded, swallowing down the swell of emotion as he took her hand and led her to the archway where the minister stood.

Taking each other's hands, they turned to the minister as he spoke. "Welcome everyone to this beautiful place to witness the marriage of Savanah Smithfield to Ramiro Perez. Having gotten to know this unique couple, one thing that became abundantly clear is that a higher power had a hand in bringing them together. They started out as children, two friends at this camp enjoying the fun, friends, and laughter that summer camp brings. As they grew into teenagers, the stirrings of young love followed them to this dock behind me, where they shared their first kiss. Then reuniting after many years as adults, their friendship very quickly grew into a deep and abiding love. Rami and Savanah, as you are surrounded by all of those that love and support you, remember this verse from the book of Peter 4:8 – Above all, love each other deeply. If you do that, a beautiful life awaits you. Have you prepared personal vows to share with each other?" he asked as they nodded, and he stepped back.

Reaching into his jacket, Rami pulled out a piece of paper, unfolded it, and let out a long exhale to steady his emotions before he began. "I thought about what I wanted to say to you today and all I kept thinking about was 80s power ballads. I started searching for lyrics to find the right words that could fully express how much I love you and the promises I want to make to you today and then I found a song I hadn't heard in years that said everything I wanted to say and more." Layne stepped up and handed Rami his guitar. He slipped the instrument over his neck and started to play. Savanah immediately recognized the tune and smiled as he serenaded her with a Starship classic. Her eyes locked on Rami's as he sang, *Nothings Gonna Stop Us Now,* she didn't notice the choir forming behind her. As the song went into the chorus, the sweet sound of children's voices joined in, making Savanah turn in surprise, her hand covering her heart. All the summer campers ranging from the age of nine to fourteen, their sweet smiling faces beaming as they sang the chorus along with Rami. Joyous tears pricked her eyes as a wave of memories washed over her. Flashbacks to the friendly little boy that comforted her that first day at camp. The night on the dock when she thought her heart would leap out of her chest when he asked if he could kiss her. The concert where their eyes met after so many years had passed. Every moment pulled together like the plot of a great love story. Their love story.

As he came to the last line of the song, the choir quieted, leaving him to sing the last line to her, his eyes radiating a love so tender she thought her heart may burst. Removing his guitar, their guests clapped as he handed it back to Layne and nodded to the choir, giving them a thumbs up before he returned his gaze to Savanah. Seeing a tear trailing down her face, he reached up and captured it with his thumb, caressing her cheek tenderly.

"I love you, Savanah, always have and always will, from now until forever."

Savanah let out a long exhale and exclaimed, "How on earth am I going to top that?"

Their guests laughed, the little giggles from the kids sounded as she turned to them, put her hand on her heart and mouthed "thank you" before bringing her attention back to Rami for her vows to him. Savanah closed her eyes a moment to steady her thoughts and emotions, opening them to meet his gaze as she spoke. "I grew up watching movies and reading books that talked about love. There was always a heroine and a protagonist that were brought together by some sort of force that neither of them could explain. Like the universe had conspired to bring them together. I never thought that kind of love really existed. I thought it was just fiction until I met you. From the first hello when we were just kids through all the firsts that followed, you have shown me that true love is real, because that's what I feel for you. Rami, I love you, always have and always will. From now until forever."

Rami squeezed her hands and smiled down at her, his eyes shiny with tears as the minister stepped forward. "Rings?"

Layne and Dee handed the minister the rings. He blessed them and handed one to Rami. Rami slipped a thin band of diamonds on her finger as he said,

"I, Ramiro, take you Savanah to be my wife. I will share my life with yours and build our dreams together, support you through times of trouble, and rejoice with you in times of happiness. I will love and respect you every day for the rest of my life. With this ring, Savanah, I marry you."

The Minister passed the ring to Savanah. As she slipped the platinum band on his finger, she said, "I, Savanah, take you Ramiro to be my husband. I will share my life with yours and build our dreams together, support you through times of trouble, and rejoice with you in times of happiness. I will love and respect you every day for the rest of my life. With this ring, Rami, I marry you."

Their smiles were wide and faces glowing with joy, the minister announced.

"By the power vested in me, by the Church of God, I now pronounce you Husband and Wife! Rami, you may kiss your bride!"

As the guests cheered and clapped, Rami drew her close, his eyes dancing in the summer sun as he dipped her back, her breath catching with surprise. "My wife," he whispered; his loving gaze locked on hers as he captured her lips for the first time as a married couple.

* * *

THE NIGHT SKY twinkled brilliantly with stars as the moon reflected on the lake. The sound of the ongoing reception echoing from the tent set up on the camp grounds. It had grown colder with the sun setting and Savanah wrapped her arms around herself as she gave into a shiver. The sound of a twig cracking and heavy footsteps on the dock made a smile tug at her lips as his familiar sandalwood scent greeted her. Warm, strong arms enrobed her as his soft lips kissed a trail up the column of her neck. She shivered again with his touch, and he removed his jacket, draping it over her shoulders.

"What are you doing out here?" he asked, turning her to face him, her arms hooking around his neck.

"I was just thinking about all those nights together, here on this dock, looking at the stars."

He smiled, the memories so vivid, as they stood on this dock together. "Now we have a lifetime of nights like this."

She sighed contentedly, looked up at the gorgeous sky full of stars, and met his loving gaze. "Can you sing my song for me?"

His mouth curved up in a grin as he brought her lips to his, their embrace sweet and tender. Pulling away, he stared deep into her eyes and started to sing her favorite song, his rich voice carrying on the summer breeze.

EPILOGUE

5 years later

"Savanah, I need you to push. Your baby's almost out." The doctor urged as nurses rushed around the delivery room.

Savanah glanced up to Rami with tired eyes, her face flushed with exertion, and he met her gaze, his brows drawn together and his soft brown eyes wet with tears. "Mi amor, you're almost done. I can see him. He's right there."

"I'm so tired." She panted, resting her head back on the pillow, her hair wet with sweat and face contorted with exhaustion. Rami smoothed her hair away from her eyes and locked his gaze on her. "Savanah, just a few more pushes. I promise. Our baby boy is almost here. I know you can do this," he encouraged her, raw emotion blanketing his face as he held back her leg.

Willing the strength to continue, she took in a deep breath, her lungs stinging, her mouth dry as she bared down and pushed. An intense pressure consumed her body as she cried out and Rami looked down, complete awe painted across his face.

"The head is out, one more push, Savanah." her doctor urged as she sucked in another strained breath and pushed one last time.

A rush of relief overtook her, and Savanah collapsed back on the bed, tears streaming down her face as the sweet cry of their newborn son filled the room. Rami kissed her head, tears spilling over as their child was placed on her chest, his sweet cry like music to her ears. Blinking away her tears, Savanah looked down at their son, his face red, eyes squinting with the light and a thick shock of curly dark hair on his head.

"He's so beautiful." She cried. Her voice was hoarse as she looked up, meeting Rami's enamored gaze. "He looks like you."

Rami leaned down and kissed their baby boy's head and caressed her cheek affectionately. "You are amazing, Mi Amor." he said before lifting her chin and lowering his lips to hers for a tender kiss.

"Mrs. Perez, can we take your son to check him out and clean him up?" a kind middle-aged nurse asked. "I promise I'll have him back to you shortly."

Savanah nodded as the nurse scooped up their baby and Rami followed the nurse as she and another younger nurse cleaned him up, checked his vitals, measured, and weighed him. Swaddling him up tight and sliding a blue cap on his head, the younger nurse returned with their son.

"7lbs 3 oz. and 21 inches long," the nurse informed as she handed the baby to Rami. "And he's beautiful and healthy. Congratulations, do you have a name?"

"Micah Hendrix Perez " Rami replied, looking at Savanah to confirm. She nodded as she beamed at their son in Rami's arms.

"Oh, I like that," the nurse replied with a smile before her gaze drifted over to Rami. "By the way, I love your new single."

Rami graciously thanked her, and Savanah shook her head. Everywhere they went, someone recognized her husband. As the wife of the lead singer of one of the hottest rock bands in Canada, she was used to all the fanfare and, after five years of marriage, had learned to take it all in stride. Even with all the acclaim, all the accolades, all the notoriety, Rami as promised remained the same incredible man she fell in love with. Grateful and humble.

After a nurse helped her with her son's first feeding, Rami changed his first diaper and now Micah was bundled up tight and cozy, fast asleep in Savanah's arms. Rami sat on the edge of the bed, gazing at his little family with so much reverence and adoration in his eyes as a smile tugged at his lips and his gaze met Savanah's. "Another first," he mused.

Savanah looked down at their beautiful boy in her arms and echoed, "Another first."

Rami reached over, caressing her cheek with tender affection. "You've made me so happy, Savanah. I love our life, our little family, and I love you more than I can express."

Deep emotion filled her chest, as there was no way to describe the love and happiness she felt looking into her husband's beautiful brown eyes. "I love you too, Rami, so much."

Rami leaned in, brushing a soft kiss to her lips, just as a nurse popped her head in, interrupting their intimate moment with a question and a smile. "Are you feeling up to some visitors? We have a waiting room full of family and friends here to see you. Can I let them in?"

Savanah nodded and looked down at her little man, sleeping peacefully in her arms.

His bandmates and their spouses entered first, flagged by Garrett, Bea, Amelia, and their two-year-old daughter Ruby. Savanah's parents followed, along with Marnie, Davis and their toddler son, Finn. Rami's parents, all his brothers and Abuela entered the room last. The room wall to wall with happy smiles. Savanah handed their sleeping son over to Rami and he proudly passed him around, the chatter and coos filling the room.

"I see this is where the party is." Dee's voice sounded as she strode into the room holding a bouquet of blue balloons, going right over to Savanah to give her a hug. "Sorry, we were at the lake when we got the call. J's just parking the truck."

Rami walked over to Dee, holding Micah. "Would his godmother like to hold him?"

Dee nodded, her eyes wide with wonder as she took their son in, and Rami lay him in her arms. Dee turned to

Savanah; her face so full of emotion as she exclaimed, "Girl, he's so beautiful!"

Savanah beamed at her best friend and glanced around the room at all the faces of those they held so dear. An overwhelming feeling of love and gratitude washed over her. Every single person in that room had loved, supported, and stood by them through everything. So many times, she thought back on their story and how they got to where they were now. It had been crazy, fun, exhilarating and at times a very difficult road to find their happiness, but there was no way she would change it. It was their story, each tiny moment like the notes in a beautiful song.

* * *

Thank you for reading Prairie Sound!
Want more steamy romance set in the idyllic small town
of Primrose?
Read Prairie Rain now!

ALSO BY TANYA RENEE

Primrose Series

Prairie Sky

Prairie Nights

Prairie Fire

Prairie Hearts

Prairie Sound

Prairie Rain

With The Band

Finding Direction

MORE FROM SERENADE PUBLISHING

Songbird

By Sarah Williams

Brigadier Station Series

By Sarah Williams:

The Brothers of Brigadier Station

The Sky over Brigadier Station

The Legacies of Brigadier Station

Christmas at Brigadier Station

Heart of the Hinterland Series

By Sarah Williams:

The Dairy Farmer's Daughter

Their Perfect Blend

Beyond the Barre

The Outback Governess (A Sweet Outback Novella)

Primrose Series

By Tanya Renee

Prairie Sky

Prairie Nights

Prairie Fire

Prairie Hearts

Prairie Sound

Prairie Rain

With The Band

Finding Direction

The Spring of Love Series

By Virginia Taylor

Forever Delighted

Forever Amused

Forever Heartfelt

The Tooth Fairy Chronicles

By Victoria Rocus

Tooth Decay With A Side Of Fae

Toothaches And Wedding Cakes

Baby Tooth And Tangled Roots

Wisdom Tooth And The Awful Truth

A New Page

by Aimee MacRae

It Happened in Paris

By Michelle Beesley

The Bondi Bubble

By Megan Krolik

White Butterfly

By Kim Foale

The Ancient Fire

By Ellen Read

The Love Healer

By A. K. Leigh

For more information visit:

www.serenadepublishing.com

ABOUT THE AUTHOR

Tanya Renee is a proud Canadian Prairie girl, who grew up on a family farm in Southeastern Manitoba Canada. Always an avid reader, she became intrigued with the romance genre at an early age when she first read Romeo and Juliet. Soon after she started to craft her own stories and poetry and by the time she was in high school, she had declared someday she would become a writer.

Married to the love of her life, she resides in Steinbach, Manitoba Canada with two teenagers and a menagerie of pets. When she's not cooking up a storm in her kitchen, she can be found tinkering in her garden, drinking copious amounts of coffee with a book in hand, listening to 80's music/audio books or at her laptop creating stories that are emotionally satisfying. She writes what she wants to read, epic stories that bring you on a journey and make you believe in love.

www.tanyareneeromance.com

ACKNOWLEDGMENTS

Firstly, I would like to thank Sarah Williams, the CEO of Serenade Publishing, for her unfailing belief in me. Your support and mentorship have helped me not only get my writing into the world but also helped me become a better writer. Thank you is never enough.

To my amazing, loyal and dedicated readers! You simply rock. Thanks for your encouragement, enthusiasm and for reading my love stories. I'm so grateful for you all.

To my husband Bart, the love of my life and my biggest fan, who always gets excited when I hand him another story to edit. You babe are the comma king! I love you Bear!

To my kids, Theo and Raina, who bring me endless joy and laughter. And who bring me pride when they add my favorite songs to their playlists. Thank you for always letting your mom belt out those songs in the car and not giving me too many eye rolls.

And lastly to all those fellow 80's and 90's rock lovers out there! I hope you geek out reading this book as much as I geeked out writing it!